"No one can twist you through a maze with as much intensity and suspense as Max Allan Collins."
    —*Clive Cussler*

"Collins is a master."
    —*Publishers Weekly*

"Collins has an outwardly artless style that conceals a great deal of art."
    —*The New York Times Book Review*

"Max Allan Collins [is] like no other writer."
    —*Andrew Vachss*

"Collins breaks out a really good one, knocking over the hard-boiled competition (Parker and Leonard for sure, maybe even Puzo) with a one-two punch: a feisty story-line told bittersweet and wry…nice and taut…the book is unputdownable. Never done better."
    —*Kirkus Reviews*

"Entertaining…full of colorful characters…a stirring conclusion."
    —*Detroit Free Press*

"Collins has a gift for creating low-life believable characters…a sharply focused action story that keeps the reader guessing till the slam-bang ending. A consummate thriller from one of the new masters of the genre."
    —*Atlanta Journal Constitution*

The ex-gangster walked into the trees, heading toward the yawning white expanse of frozen water. I followed behind, nine millimeter in one hand, sawed-off in the other.

As we wound through the pines, the snow got deeper, ankle deep in places. Finally, at the snowy edge of the wooded shore, Harry came to a stop, and half turned.

"Go on, Harry."

Harry frowned. "Go on? What the fuck, 'go on?' "

"Keep walking."

"Where?"

I gestured with the shotgun, toward the lake.

Harry followed the gesture, eyes tight, and it took a few seconds for him to absorb the meaning. Somehow, though, he couldn't turn his confusion and apprehension into words.

Harry looked at the lake, then at me; the lake, me.

His voice seemed even higher pitched than before, almost childish, his wide eyes buggy behind the lenses. "What...what if the ice gives, under me? I mean...it's gonna get thin, farther out I get...."

"We'll keep the stress to a minimum."

"How?"

"I'll stay put," I said...

The Last QUARRY·

by **Max Allan Collins**

A HARD CASE CRIME NOVEL

A HARD CASE CRIME BOOK
(HCC-023)
August 2006

Published by

Dorchester Publishing Co., Inc.
200 Madison Avenue
New York, NY 10016

in collaboration with Winterfall LLC

ISBN 0-8439-5593-7

For Jeffrey Goodman—
who brought my killer
to life

"Any victim demands allegiance."
Graham Greene

THE LAST QUARRY

One

It had been a long time since I'd had any trouble sleeping.

Not since the fucking shelling was keeping me awake, a lifetime or two ago. I'm not by nature an insomniac. You might think killing people for a living would give you some bad nights. Truth is, guys in the killing biz? Just aren't the type to be bothered.

I was no exception. I hadn't gone into retirement because my conscience was bothering me. I retired because I had enough money put away to live comfortably without working, so I did. And for a while that retirement had gone well. I'd invested a little and was living off the gravy; I'd even been married for a while, which had worked out fine.

For a while.

Currently I was deposited in an A-frame cottage with a deck onto the frozen expanse of Sylvan Lake, somewhere in Minnesota, only it's not called Sylvan Lake and maybe it's not Minnesota, either. I was staying at the only resort on this side of the lake, Sylvan Lodge, but I was not a guest—I ran the place. Or, anyway, did when it wasn't off-season.

Once upon a time I had owned a resort in Wisconsin

not unlike this—not near the acreage, of course, and not near the occupancy; but I had *owned* the place, whereas here I was just the manager.

Of course I didn't have anything to complain about. I was lucky to have the job. When I ran into Gary Petersen in Milwaukee, where he was attending a convention and I was making a one-night stopover to remove some emergency funds from several bank deposit boxes, I was at the loosest of loose ends. The name I'd lived under for over a decade was unusable; my past had caught up with me, back at Paradise Lake, where everything went to hell in an instant: my straight business yanked from under me, my wife (who'd had not a clue of my prior existence) murdered in her sleep.

Gary, however, had recognized me in the hotel bar and called out a name I hadn't used since the early '70s: my real one.

"Jack!" he said, only that wasn't the name. For the purposes of this narrative, however, we'll say my real name is Jack Keller.

"Gary," I said, surprised by the warmth creeping into my voice. "You son of a bitch…you're still alive."

Gary was a huge man—six six, weighing in at somewhere between three hundred pounds and a ton; his face was masked in a bristly brown beard, his skull exposed by hair loss, his dark eyes bright, his smile friendly, in a goofy, almost child-like way.

"Thanks to you, asshole," he said.

We'd been in Vietnam together.

"What the hell have you been doing all these years, Jack?"

"Mostly killing people."

He boomed a laugh. "Yeah, right!"

"Don't believe me, then."

I was, incidentally, pretty drunk. I don't drink often, but I'd been through the mill lately.

"Are you crying, Jack?"

"Fuck no," I said.

But I was.

Gary slipped his arm around my shoulder; it was like getting cuddled by God. "Bro—what's the deal? What shit have you been through?"

"They killed my wife," I said, and blubbered drunkenly into his shoulder.

"Jesus, Jack—who...?"

"Fucking assholes...fucking assholes...."

We went to his suite. He was supposed to play poker with some buddies but he called it off.

I was very drunk and very morose and Gary was, at one time anyway, my closest friend, and during the most desperate of days.

I told him everything.

I told him how after I got back from Nam, I found my wife—my first wife—shacked up with some guy, some fucking auto mechanic, who was working under a car when I kicked the jack out. The jury let me off, but I was finished in my hometown, and I drifted until the Broker found me. The Broker, who gave me the name Quarry, was the conduit through whom the murder-for-hire contracts came, and, what? Ten years later the Broker was dead, by my hand, and I was out of the killing business and took my savings and went to Paradise Lake in Wisconsin, where eventually I met a pleasant, attractive, not terribly bright woman and she and I were in the lodge business until the past came looking for me, and suddenly she was dead, and I was without a life or even identity. I had managed to kill the fuckers responsible for my wife's killing—political assholes, not wiseguys—but otherwise I had nothing. Nothing left but some money stashed away, that I was now retrieving.

I told Gary all this, through the night, in considerably more detail though probably even less coherently, although coherently enough that when I woke up the next morning, where Gary had laid me out on the extra bed, I knew I'd told him too much.

He was still asleep. Like me, he was in the same clothes we'd worn to that bar; like me, he smelled of booze, only he also reeked of cigarette smoke. I reeked a little, too, but it was Gary's smoke: I never picked up the habit. Bad for you.

He looked like a big dead animal, except for his barrel-like chest heaving with breath. I looked at this man—like me, he was somewhere near or past fifty, not the kids we'd been before the war made us worse than just men.

I still had liquor in me, but I was sober now. Too deadly fucking sober. I studied my best-friend-of-long-ago and wondered if I had to kill him.

I was standing over him, staring down at him, mulling that over, when his eyes opened suddenly, like a timer turning on the lights in a house to fend off burglars. He smiled a little, then it faded, his eyes narrowed, and he said, "Morning, Jack."

"Morning, Gary."

"You've got that look."

"What look is that?"

"The cold one. The one I first saw a long time ago."

I swallowed and took my eyes off him. Sat on the edge of the bed across from him and rubbed my eyes with the heels of my hands.

He plopped down across from me with those big paws on his big knees and said, "How the hell d'you manage it?"

"What?"

"Hauling my fat ass onto that Medivac."

I grunted a laugh. "The same way a little mother lifts a Buick off her big baby."

"In my case, you lifted the Buick onto the baby. Let me buy you breakfast."

"Okay."

In the hotel coffee shop, he said, "Funny…what you told me last night…about the business you used to be in?"

I sipped my coffee; I didn't look at him—didn't show him my eyes. "Yeah?"

"I'm in the same game."

Now I looked at him; I winced with disbelief. "What…?"

He corrected my initial thought. "The tourist game, I mean. I run a lodge near Brainerd."

"No kidding."

"That's what this convention is. Northern Resort Owners Association."

"I heard of it," I said, nodding. "Never bothered to join, myself."

Not by nature much of a joiner.

"I'm a past president," he said, obviously proud of that. "Anyway, I run a place called Sylvan Lodge. My third and current, and I swear to God everlasting wife, Ruth Ann? Maybe I mentioned her last night? Anyway, Ruthie inherited it from her late parents, God rest their hardworking Republican souls."

None of this came as a surprise to me. Grizzly bear Gary had always drawn women like a great big magnet—usually good-looking little women who wanted a father figure, Papa Bear variety. Even in

Bangkok on R & R, Gary never had to pay for pussy, as we used to delicately phrase it.

"I'm happy for you," I said. "I always figured you'd manage to marry for money."

"My ass! I really love Ruth Ann. You should see the knockers on the child."

"A touching testimonial if I ever heard one. Listen… about that bullshit I was spouting last night…"

His dark eyes became slits, the smile in his brushy face disappeared. "We'll never speak of that again. Understood? Never."

He reached out and squeezed my forearm.

I sighed and smiled tightly and nodded, relieved. Killing Gary would have been no fun at all.

He continued, though. "My sorry fat ass wouldn't even be on this planet, if it wasn't for you. I owe you big time."

"Bullshit," I said, but not very convincingly.

"I've had a good life, at least the last ten years or so, since I met Ruthie. You've been swimming in Shit River long enough. Let me help you out."

"Gary, I…"

"Actually, I want *you* to help *me*."

"Help you?"

Gary's business was such a thriving one that he had recently invested in a second lodge, one across the way from his Gull Lake resort. He had quickly discovered he couldn't run both places himself, at least not "without running my fat ass off." He offered me the job of managing Sylvan.

"We'll start you at 5OK, with free housing. You can make a tidy buck with damn near no overhead, and you can tap into at least one of your marketable skills, and at the same time be out of the way. Keep as low a profile as you like. You don't even have to deal with the tourists, to speak of—we have a social director for that. You just keep the boat afloat. Okay?"

"Okay," I said, and we shook hands.

Goddamn I was glad I hadn't killed him....

Two

Now, here I was a little more than six months into the job, and a month into the first winter—off-season, settled in. My quarters, despite the rustic trappings of the cabin-like exterior, were modern—pine paneling skirting the room with pale yellow pastel walls rising to a high pointed ceiling. Just one A-frame room with bath and kitchenette, but a big room, facing the lake, which was a mere hundred yards from the deck that was my back porch. Couch, Dish TV, plenty of closet space, a comfortable bed. I didn't need anything more.

During off-season like this, I could've moved into more spacious digs if I liked, but I hadn't bothered. My first summer and fall at Sylvan Lodge had been a real pleasure. Just a short jog across the way was an indoor swimming pool with hot tub and sauna, plus a tennis court; a golf course, shared with Gary's other lodge, was an easy drive. My duties were constant, but mostly consisted of delegating authority, and the gay chef of our gourmet restaurant made sure I ate well and free, and I'd been banging Nikki, the college girl who had the social director position for the summer, so my staff relations were solid.

But the cold months had come, and in this part of the world that was fucking cold indeed. Everyone except a maintenance guy, José, was gone, and even he didn't live on site; Nikki was back blowing frat boys and probably posing for a *Playboy* college-girl spread, and I didn't even want to know what my gay chef was up to. Gary was off with Ruth Ann down in Florida, where his "winter" home was, and I was up here, keeping an eye on things—like making sure a moose didn't get inside the restaurant and take a dump or something.

In short, I had nothing to do. The only managerial instruction I'd given José since we closed for the season was to keep the pool and hot tub and sauna going, for my personal use.

So for the past month, boredom had started to itch at me…and for the past few nights I'd had trouble sleeping. I sat up all night watching satellite TV and reading paperback westerns; then I'd drag around the next day, maybe drifting to sleep in the afternoon just long enough to fuck up my sleep cycle again that night.

It was getting irritating.

At about three-thirty in the morning on the fourth night of this shit, I decided eating might do the trick. Fill my gut with junk food and the blood could rush down from my head and warm my belly and I'd get the fuck sleepy, finally. I hadn't tried this before because I'd been getting a trifle paunchy, with this easy job, even more so since winter kicked in.

In the summer, at least, I could swim in the lake every day and get some exercise and keep the fucking spare tire off. But with winter here, I'd just let my beard go and belt size, too. I tried to make myself do laps in the pool across the way, but mostly I sat in the hot tub and drank Coca Cola and thought about my past. I wasn't sure why—it wasn't the kind of past you got anywhere with by thinking about it. The only thing I knew for sure was, this winter was making me fat and lazy and, now, fucking sleepless.

The cupboard was bare so I threw on my thermal jacket and—since I was alone on my stretch of Sylvan Lake—took the ten-mile ride to the nearest junk food. At this time of night a shabby little convenience store, Ray's Mart, with its one self-service gas pump, was the only thing open fifteen miles in either direction.

The clerk was a heavy-set brunette named Cindy from Brainerd. She was maybe twenty years old and a little surly, but she worked all night, so who could blame her.

"Mr. Ryan," she said, flatly, as I came in, the bell over the door jingling. She was engrossed in a telephone conversation and this effusive greeting had been both an effort and a concession to a regular customer.

"Cindy," I said, with a nod, and I began prowling the place, three narrow aisles parallel to the front of the building. None of the snacks appealed to me—chips and crackers and Twinkies and other preservative-packed delights—and the frozen food case ran mostly to ice-cream sandwiches and popsicles. In this weather, that was a joke.

I was giving a box of Chef Boyardee lasagna an intent once-over, like it was a car I was considering buying, when the bell over the door jingled again. I glanced up and saw a well-dressed, heavy-set man—heavy-set enough to make Cindy look svelte—with a pockmarked, Uncle Fester-ish face and black-rimmed glasses that fogged up as soon as he stepped in.

He wore an expensive topcoat—a tan Burberry number with a red-and-black plaid scarf, the sort of pricey ensemble that required a small mortgage—and his shoes had a bright black city shine, barely flecked with ice and snow. His name was Harry Something-the-fuck, and he was from Chicago. I knew him, in my former life.

I turned my back.

If he saw me, I'd have to kill him—I was bored, but not that bored.

Predictably, Harry Something went straight for the potato chips; he also rustled around the area where cookies were shelved. I risked a glimpse and saw him, not two minutes after he entered, with his arms full of junk food, heading for the front counter.

"Excuse me, miss," Harry Something said, depositing his groceries before Cindy like an offering on an altar. His voice was nasal and high-pitched; a funny, childish voice for a man his size—it went well with the Uncle Fester face. "Could you direct me to the sanitary napkins?"

Cindy winced, phone in hand, annoyed by this intrusion. Harry was not a regular customer.

She said, "You mean Tampax?"

"Whatever."

"Toiletries is just over there."

Now this was curious, and I'll tell you why. I had met Harry Something around ten years before, when I was doing a job for the Outfit boys in Chicago. I was never a mob guy, mind you, strictly a freelancer, but their money was as good as anybody's. What that job was isn't important, but Harry and his partner Louis were the locals who had fucked up, making my outsider's presence necessary. Harry and Louis had not been friendly toward me. They had threatened me, in fact. They had beaten the hell out of me in my hotel room, when the job was over, for making them look bad.

I had never taken any sort of revenge out on them. I occasionally do take revenge, but at my convenience, and only when a score strikes me as worth settling. Harry and Louis had really just pushed me around a little, bloodied my nose, tried to earn back a little self-respect. So I didn't hold a grudge. Not a major grudge. Fuck it.

As to why Harry Something purchasing Tampax in the middle of the night at some backwoods convenience store was curious, well, Harry and Louis were gay. Like my old man used to say, queer as a three-dollar bill. Mob muscle who worked as a pair, and played as a pair.

And I don't mean to be critical. To each his own. I'd rather cut off my dick than insert it in any orifice of a repulsive fat slob like Harry Something. But, hey, that's just me.

Now while I'm as naturally curious as the next guy, I'm sure as hell not nosy, not even inquisitive, really. But when a faggot buys Tampax, you have to wonder why.

"Excuse me," Harry Something said, brushing by me.

He hadn't seen my face (had he?)—and he might not recognize me, in any case. Ten years and a beard and twenty pounds later, I wasn't as easy to peg as Harry was, who had changed goddamn little.

Harry, having stocked up on cookies and chips and Tampax, was now buying milk and packaged macaroni and cheese and provisions in general. He was shopping.

Stocking up.

And now I was starting to get a handle on what he might be up to....

I nodded to surly Cindy, who bid me goodbye by flickering her eyelids in casual contempt, and went out to my car, a steel-gray Jag I'd purchased recently. I wished I'd had the Lodge's four-wheel drive, or anything less conspicuous, but I didn't. I sat in the car, scooched down low; I did not turn on the engine. I just sat in the cold car in the cold night and waited.

Harry Something came out with two armloads of groceries—Tampax included, I presumed—and he put them in the front seat of a brown rental Ford Taurus. Louis was not waiting in the car for him.

Harry was alone.

Which further confirmed my suspicions....

I waited for him to pull out onto the road, hung back till he took the road's curve, then started up my Jag and glided out after him. He had turned left, toward Brainerd. That made sense, only I figured he wouldn't wind up there—he'd likely light out for the boonies somewhere.

I knew what Harry was up to, vaguely at least. He sure as shit wasn't here to ski—that lardass couldn't stand up on a pair of skis. And he wasn't here to go ice-fishing, either. A city boy like Harry Something had no business in a touristy area like this, in the off-season...

...unless Harry was hiding out, holing up somewhere.

This would be the perfect area for that.

Only Harry didn't use Tampax.

He turned off on a side road, into a heavily wooded area that wound back toward Sylvan Lake.

Good. That was very good.

I went on by. I drove a mile, turned into a farmhouse gravel drive and headed back without lights. I slowed as I reached the mouth of the side road, and could see Harry's taillights wink off.

I knew the cabin at the end of that road. There was only one, and its owner only used it during the summer; Harry was either a renter, or a squatter.

I glided on by and went back home.

I left the Jag next to the deck and walked up the steps and into the A-frame. The nine millimeter Browning was in the nightstand drawer. The gun hadn't been shot in months—Christ, maybe over a year. But I cleaned and oiled it regularly, because you never know.

It would do nicely.

So would my black turtleneck, black jeans, black leather bomber jacket, and this black moonless night. I slipped a spare .38 revolver in the bomber jacket right side pocket, and clipped a hunting knife to my belt. The knife was razor sharp with a sword point; I sent for it out of the back of one of those dumb-ass mercenary magazines—which are worthless except for mail-ordering weapons.

I walked along the edge of the lake, my running shoes crunching the brittle ground, layered as it was with snow and ice and leaves. The only light came from a gentle scattering of stars, a handful of diamonds flung on black velvet; the frozen lake was a dark presence that you could sense but not really see, the surrounding trees even darker. The occasional cabin or cottage or house I passed was empty. I was one of only a handful of residents on this side of Sylvan Lake who were staying year-round.

But the lights were on in one cabin. Not many lights, but lights. And its chimney was trailing smoke.

The cabin was small, a traditional log cabin of the Abe Lincoln and syrup variety, only with a satellite dish. Probably two bedrooms, a living room, kitchenette and a can or two. Only one car—the brown rental Ford.

My footsteps were lighter now; I was staying on the balls of my feet and the crunching under them was faint. I approached with caution and gun in hand and peeked in a window on the right front side.

Harry Something was sitting on the couch, eating corn curls, giving himself an orange mustache in the process. His feet were up on a coffee table. More food and a sawed-off double-barreled shotgun were on the couch next to him. He wore a colorful Hawaiian shirt; he looked like Don Ho puked on him, actually.

In the nearby kitchenette, which was open onto the living room, Louis was fussing as he put the food away—a small, skinny, bald ferret of man, who wore jeans and a black shirt and a white tie. I couldn't tell whether he was trying for trendy or gangster, and frankly didn't give a shit.

Physically, all the two men had in common was pockmarks and a desire for the other's ugly body.

And neither one of them seemed to need a tampon, though a towelette would've come in handy for Harry Something. Jesus. Imagine having a Burberry topcoat like that and a Hawaiian shirt underneath; they can make gay marriage legit if they want to, but *that* should be fucking illegal.

I could hear them talking—muffled but audible through the window, the sound of the television, some old movie, underneath.

From the couch Harry said, "Chip me!"

From the kitchenette Louis said, "With *your* cholesterol? Isn't a bag of cheese curls *enough*?"

"Don't mama me!…I wanna Coke, too."

"I thought you were *off* caffeine!"

"Not when you expect me to sit up all fuckin' night."

Louis was in the living room now. "*I'm* the one *dealing* with her—what a spoiled little cunt *she* is!"

Harry laughed; the laugh was like Uncle Fester, too. "That's why daddy'll pay up, sweet cheeks!"

I peeked at them—Louis was delivering barbecue chips and Harry took them with a "Thank you," and they interrupted their bickering to exchange fond expressions. Then Harry worked at adding a new shade of orange to his junk-food mustache.

Me, I huddled back down beneath the window, wondering what I was doing here.

Boredom, for sure.

Curiosity, maybe.

I shrugged. Time to look in another window or two.

Because Harry and Louis clearly had a captive, and a female one at that. That's what they were doing in the boonies. That's why they were stocking up on supplies at a convenience store in the middle of night and nowhere. That's why there were in the market for Tampax.

And through a back window, I saw her.

She was on a single bed in the small rustic room, naked but for white panties—a wrist cuffed to a nearby bedpost, sitting on the edge of the bed, bending over in obvious discomfort, crying...a dark-haired, creamy-fleshed beauty in her early twenties, suffering menstrual cramps.

Obviously, Harry and Louis had nothing sexual in mind for this captive; the reason for her nudity was to help prevent her fleeing. The bed was heavy with blankets, and she'd clearly been keeping under the covers, but right now she was sitting and doubling over and crying. Right now was a bad period for her any way you sliced it.

Thing was, I recognized this young woman. Like Harry, I spent a lot of hours during cold nights like this with my eyes frozen to a TV screen. And that's where I'd seen her: on the tube.

Not an actress, no—an heiress. Jonah Green's daughter—"Daddy" was a Chicago media magnate whose name you'd recognize if I was using his real one, a guy who inherited money and wheeled-and-dealed his way into more, including one of the satellite super-stations I'd been wasting my eyes on lately. The Windy City's answer to Ted Turner, right down to sailboating and baseball teams and womanizing.

His daughter was a little wild—seen in the company of rock stars (she had a tattoo of a star—not Justin Timberlake, a five-pointed star—on her white left breast, which I could see from the window) and was a Betty Ford clinic drop-out. Nonetheless, she was said to be the apple of her daddy's eye, even if that apple was a tad wormy.

So Harry and Louis had put the snatch on the snatch; fair enough. Question was, was it their own idea, or something the Outfit put them up to?

I heard a door open, and peeked in carefully, just barely able to hear the muffled speech through the window.

Louis came in and tossed the box of Tampax in her lap.

The girl snarled, "You took long enough!"

"We're being nice—*you* be nice."

"Fuck you. Fuck you!…I need the bathroom."

A clearly disgusted Louis dug a handcuff key out of his pocket, and worked at undoing her wrist.

The girl, a spoiled brat even in the presence of kidnappers, said, "Hurry the fuck up, faggot! You want blood everywhere?"

He looked at her coldly. "Do you?"

That sobered her a little.

Maybe Daddy should've tried some of Louis's brand of psychology.

Then Louis walked her off somewhere as the girl clutched the Tampax box like treasure.

I dropped down from the window, hidden there in the dark in my dark clothes with a gun in my hand and my back to the log cabin, and I smiled.

When I'd come out into the night, armed like this, it hadn't been to effect a rescue. Whatever else they were, Harry and Louis were dangerous men, and I had to be ready to protect my ass. And if I was going to spend my sleepless night satisfying my curiosity and assuaging my boredom by poking into their business, I had to be ready to pay for my thrills.

So I sat in the cold and dark and decided, finally, that it just didn't matter who or what was behind it.

My options were to go home, and forget about it, and try (probably without any luck) to get some sleep; or to rescue this somewhat soiled damsel in distress.

And if I went home, they'd kill this girl.

What the hell. I had nothing better to do.

I went to the front door and knocked.

No answer.

Shit, I knew somebody was home, so I knocked again.

Then I got right against the door, putting my ear to the wood, so I could gauge their reaction within....

Harry was saying, "Who the fuck is *that*? Who could that be?"

Louis was calming him, saying, "Could be that security company the owner told us about—on patrol. Saw lights on."

TV sound stopped—muted.

Harry's voice again: "You want me to—"

"No! Hide the shottie...."

"Louis, no one knows we're *here*...."

"That's right—nothing to worry about."

Louis cracked open the door and peered out and said, "What is it?" and I shot him in the eye.

Three

The still night was cut by the harsh, shrill sound of a scream—not Louis, who hadn't had time for that, but the girl in the next room, scared shitless at hearing a gunshot, one would suppose.

I paid no attention to her and shouldered the door open—no night latch or anything—and stepped over Louis, kicked aside the .38 revolver he'd been hiding behind him when he answered the door, and moved into the claustrophobic living room, pointing the nine millimeter at Harry, whose orange-ringed mouth was frozen open and whose bag of barbecue potato chips dropped to the floor, much as Louis had.

"Don't, Harry," I said.

I could see in Harry's tiny dark eyes behind his thick black-rimmed glasses that he was thinking about the sawed-off shotgun under the pillow on the couch next to him.

"Who the fuck…?"

I moved slowly to the couch; behind me, an old colorized movie was playing on their captive's daddy's superstation. With my left hand, I plucked the shotgun from under the cushion next to Harry and tucked it under my arm.

"Hi, Harry," I said. "Been a while."

His orange-ringed mouth slowly began to work and his eyes began to blink and he said, "Quarry?"

That was the name he'd known me by.

His eyes showed white all around and he pointed at me. "You're that fucker *Quarry!*"

I dipped down to pluck the .38 from the floor. "Taking the girl your idea, or are you still working for the boys?"

His words came to him from some remote part of his brain, a response not unlike the kick from a doctor-applied mallet to a knee. "We...we retired, couple years ago. God."

He looked past me, wide-eyed, at the thing on the floor and pointed again, this time like a kid in the backseat who just spotted a Dairy Queen. But not as happy.

"You...you killed...Jesus Christ, you killed *Louis*...!"

I sat on the arm of the sofa and kept the gun on him, casually but on him. "Right. What were you going to put the girl's body in?"

"Huh?"

"She's obviously seen you. You were obviously going to kill her, once you got the money. So. What was the plan?"

Harry wiped off his orange barbecue ring with a hand. He was blinking, trying to think. "Got a roll of plastic in the closet. Gonna roll her up and dump her in one of them gravel pits they got around here."

"I see. Do that number with the plastic right now, with Louis, why don't you? Okay?"

Tears were rolling down Harry's chubby, stubbly pockmarked cheeks. I didn't know whether he was crying for Louis or himself or the pair of them, and I wasn't interested enough to ask.

"Okay," he said thickly, apparently resigned to his fate, his mouth slack but his eyes moving with thought.

I watched him roll his partner up in the sheet of plastic, using duct tape to secure the package; he sobbed as he did it, but he did it. He got blood on his Hawaiian shirt; it didn't particularly show, though.

"Good job, Harry. Now…I want you to clean up the mess. Go on. You'll find what you need in the kitchen."

Dutifully, Harry shuffled over to where the open kitchen met the little living room, got a pan of warm water and some rags, and dropped to his knees to clean up the brains and blood. He wasn't crying anymore. He moved slow but steady, a fat zombie in a colorful shirt.

"Stick the rags in the end of the plastic there, Harry, would you? Thank you."

Harry did that, then the big man lumbered to

his feet, hands half-heartedly in the air, and said, "Now me?"

"I might let you go, Harry. I got nothing against you."

His eyes jumped. "Not…not how I remember it."

I laughed. "You girls leaned on me once. You think I'd kill a person over something that trivial? What kind of asshole do you think I am, Harry?"

Harry had sense enough not to answer.

"Let's see how Daddy's little girl's doing," I said, and with the nine millimeter's nose kissing Harry's neck, I walked him to the door of the bedroom.

"Open it," I said.

He did.

We went in, Harry first.

The girl was under the covers, holding the blankets and sheets up around her in a combination of illogical modesty and legitimate fear.

Her expression melted into confusion mingled with the beginnings of hope, when she saw me.

"Everything's going to be all right, Miss Green," I told her. "I've already taken care of the skinny one." I nudged Harry with the gun in his neck. "You got a handcuff key?"

Harry swallowed and nodded.

"Uncuff her."

My gun trained on him from nearby, Harry was complying as she asked, "Did…did my Daddy send you?"

I held out my hand to Harry and he dropped the cuff key in my palm.

"Fatso and me are taking a moonlight stroll," I told her. "Meantime, you stay put. I'm going to get you back to your father."

Her confusion didn't leave, but she began to smile, wide, a kid Christmas morning, seeing her gifts. Her gift to me was dropping the blankets and sheets to her waist. The cute cupcake breasts had pierced nipples with rings, like beer cans waiting to be opened.

"Remember," I said, and waggled a teacherly finger. "Stay right there."

She swallowed and nodded and her eyes sparkled. Well, they did.

I walked my host out, pulling the bedroom door shut behind me.

"Where are her clothes, Harry?"

He nodded to a closet. Same one he'd gotten the plastic out of.

"Good," I said. "Now let's go for a walk. Just the three of us."

Harry frowned in confusion, glanced back toward the bedroom. "Girl's comin'?"

"No. Louis. Better give him a hand."

Now Harry got it.

He leaned down and hefted his partner in the plastic shroud and held the crinkly corpse in his arms like a B-movie monster carrying a starlet. The plastic was spattered with blood, but only on the inside; you could sort of see what was left of Louis's head trying to look out. Harry seemed like he was going to cry again.

I still had the sawed-off shotgun under my arm, so it was awkward, getting the front door open.

Cold came in, but I barely noticed. I don't think Harry much noticed, either.

"What…?" he asked. "Where…?"

"Out on the lake," I said, and nodded in that direction.

"…can I get my coat?"

"I don't think so. I think the cold will keep you on your toes, and anyway, suppose you have a gun in your pocket, and I have to kill you, and mess up that beautiful Burberry. Which would be a fucking shame, plus which I'd have to make two trips, carrying Louis, and your fat ass."

He swallowed, nodded, as if all that sounded reasonable enough. "Okay. I…there's a shovel I could get…?"

"We won't need it. Ground's too hard, anyway."

Harry looked at me, his eyes behind the glasses wary, glancing from me to his plastic-wrapped burden and back again.

I responded to the question his face was asking: "We're going to bury Louis at sea."

"Huh?"

Now I was noticing the cold. "Outside, Harry. My

nipples are getting hard, and not in a good way. Okay? Outside."

He moved past me, his plastic bundle over one shoulder—he might have been delivering a rug.

The chubby ex-gangster walked into the trees, heading toward the yawning white expanse of frozen water. I followed behind, nine millimeter in one hand, sawed-off in the other. Harry in his Hawaiian shirt was an oddly comic sight, but I was too busy to be amused.

As we wound through the pines, the snow got deeper, ankle deep in places. As his glasses got unfogged and made his trek easier, Harry made conversation.

"Was...was that you, Quarry? Back at that fucking convenience store?"

"That's right."

"And, what? You...you thought we'd come after you? This has nothing to do with you."

"Does now. And anyway, I got my question answered."

He risked a frown back at me. "What question?"

"What the Odd Couple needs with Tampax in the middle of the night....Keep moving."

Finally, at the snowy edge of the wooded shore, Harry came to a stop, and half turned, Louis turning too, Harry asking another question with his face: *What now?*

"Go on, Harry."

Harry frowned. "Go on? What the fuck, 'go on?' "

"Keep walking."

"*Where?*"

I gestured with the shotgun, toward the lake.

Harry followed the gesture, eyes tight, and it took a few seconds for him to absorb the meaning. Somehow, though, he couldn't turn his confusion and apprehension into words.

So I said, "When you sense the ice getting thin, give Louis a toss...let the lake have him. Then head back here, and we'll talk."

Harry looked at the lake, then at me; the lake, me.

His voice seemed even higher pitched than before, almost childish, his wide eyes buggy behind the lenses. "What...what if the ice gives, under me? I mean...it's gonna get thin, farther out I get...."

"We'll keep the stress to a minimum."

"*How?*"

"I'll stay put."

All the air went out of Harry, and if Louis had been one pound heavier, both men would have gone down in a pile in the snow, right there. But he stayed on his feet, even though the despair must have been heavier than Louis.

"Quarry...Quarry...will you just fuckin' kill me. Kill me here and be done."

I shrugged. "Thought you might like a sporting chance, Harry. Before you know it, you'll be out of range…maybe you can make it over to those trees, where I can't catch up with you."

He summoned a sneer from somewhere. "If the ice don't break first."

I shrugged again. "That's between you and the ice."

He sneered at me; but the sneer dissolved into this pitiful, lower-lip trembling thing that got only a single shake of the head out of me. That, and another nod toward the lake.

Cradling Louis like a groom carrying a bride across the threshold (which was fitting, as Louis had been the wife), Harry heaved a sigh, took a tentative step, and found the ice firm. He drew a deep breath, as if he were diving into water, not about to walk on the frozen variety, and then he was making his way with the mummy-like bundle out onto the lake, walking carefully, hesitantly, testing the ice with one baby step after another, always letting the tentative ground settle under him.

It took a long time—maybe two minutes. Harry would look at his feet, then off to the bank on the right and the thick darkness of trees, clearly considering that option. His breath was visible, small puffy clouds, and the heavy sound of it came back over the stillness of the lake, interrupted only by the call of a loon. Or something—some damn bird too stupid to fly the fuck south.

Subtle at first, the cracking seemed something I was only imagining, in my anticipation; but Harry had heard it, too, because he was poised out there as frozen as the lake.

Actually, more frozen, because suddenly the ice was snapping under his shoes, as if he were standing on a window, and that window was breaking....

He didn't even have time to run. He was clutching onto Louis, which might have been bittersweet, only I think he was hoping he could use Louis like a big piece of driftwood or something, but it didn't work out that way.

Louis disappeared, sliding under like a turd down the crapper, leaving Harry to flail, and try to hold onto the bigger chunks of ice; he was screaming my name and swearing, then the splashing was louder than the screaming and then the screaming stopped altogether and finally the splashing subsided.

And he was gone.

I studied the lake—soon you could barely see the hole Harry had made—with the black starry sky my only companion. Even the loon had nothing to say, the frozen expanse and the surrounding blackness of trees as quiet as, well, death. Suddenly this wintry world seemed austerely beautiful to me, a study in white and gray and gray-blue and black, but enjoying myself like that seemed vaguely creepy, so I headed back to the cabin, shotgun slung over my arm.

Back inside, I got the girl's clothes out of the closet—her cell phone was in a pocket—and went in and gave them to her, keeping the phone. A black hip-hop t-shirt and designer jeans and Reeboks.

"Did you kill those men?" she said, breathlessly, her eyes dark and glittering. She had her clothes in her lap.

"That's not important. Get dressed."

"You're wonderful. You're goddamn fucking wonderful."

"I know," I said. "Everybody says so. Get dressed."

She got dressed.

I watched her.

She was a beautiful piece of ass, no question, and even with those rings in them, the titties were cute as puppy dogs. The way she was looking at me made it clear she was grateful.

I said, "We need to call your father."

"What's your hurry? After a *reward*? There's all kinds of rewards...."

I held her cell phone out to her. "We should call him."

She shrugged and came at me and I found myself backed against the wall, as if she were holding a gun on me. Then her arms were around me and the pretty little mug was looking up at me devilishly.

She had to get up on tiptoes to do it, but she kissed me long and slow and her tongue knew things it shouldn't have at her age.

Then she drew away from me, her arms still around me. "What do you say, hero?"

"Kind of a bad time, isn't it?"

Her eyes flashed. "I think it's exciting."

"I mean...of the month."

That made her laugh. She raised an eyebrow. "Other ports in a storm...?"

"Maybe later," I said, and smiled.

She looked like AIDS-bait to me. I could be reckless, but not that reckless.

Disappointed, she took a step away and accepted the cell phone, and within seconds was saying, "Daddy?...I'm fine, I'm fine...yes!...Daddy, you know that *man* you sent...what?"

She frowned up at me in confusion. "He says...he says he didn't send anybody."

I gestured impatiently for the phone and she gave it to me.

"Good evening, sir. I have your daughter. As you can hear, she's just fine....Get together one hundred thousand dollars in unmarked, non-sequential tens, twenties and fifties, and wait for the next call."

I hung up.

She looked at me with wide eyes and wide-open mouth.

"Relax," I told her. "I'm not going to kill you—just turning a buck."

"You bastard! You *prick!*"

She spit in my face.

I wiped it off with a hand and gave her a look.

She started backing up, her eyes wild, and I got hold of her, carried the squirming creature back to her bed and dumped her there.

I thrust a stern finger in that cute face. "Look! I gotta get some sleep. Pipe down, or I'll duct-tape your little trap."

She behaved after that, though she cried and sniffled and tried to make me feel as sorry for her as she did for herself, which would have been impossible; on the other hand, some of it was genuine—she did have cramps. I cuffed her to the bedpost and she was able to recline. I even covered her up.

Then I went over and curled up on the other bed, nine millimeter in my waistband.

I'd taken some risks tonight.

I lived and worked on this lake, after all. But it was winter, and the bodies wouldn't turn up for a long time, if ever, and the Outfit had used this part of the world to dump its corpses since Capone was just a mean street kid. Very little chance any of this would come back at me. And killing Harry and Louis had, at least, killed my insomnia.

For the first time in a long time…

…I slept like a baby.

Four

The Log Cabin, true to its name, was a log cabin, a roadside gas station and latter-day diner a good hundred miles from Lake Sylvan, a minor intrusion of civilization into a world of snowy pines. At eleven A.M., breakfast was a memory and lunch the future, so the graveled parking lot was home to only a couple of cars and two trucks.

I was keeping watch through binoculars on the slope across the two-lane highway, sheltered and concealed by more of those snowy pines; the ground had only a dusting of snow but the air was brittle with cold. I'd left the ninja-black wardrobe home—in daylight, it would have only made me stand out against the winter whiteness—and was in work boots and jeans and a brown corduroy fleece-lined jacket that were comfortable enough. I'd been keeping tabs on this ransom drop for half an hour already, and it took that long for the girl to speak.

"He won't come himself, you know."

Julie Green was seated like an Indian, leaning back against a big nearby tree, looking utterly bored, an old brown leather jacket of mine loose over her shoulders, her nipples perked under the black hip-hop t-shirt that peeked out, her designer jeans brushed with snow, her handcuffed hands in her lap.

Basically, she looked like a surly high school student waiting outside the principal's office.

"Well, Daddy *should* come," I said, "if he has any use for you. Those were the terms."

She shrugged and smirked. Her teeth chattered now and then. "He doesn't have much use for me. Plus, don't ever forget—he's a lying untrustworthy shit."

I lifted the binoculars again. "Good to know."

A money-green Lexus was pulling in, taking one of half a dozen stalls next to the restaurant. I re-focused the binoculars and watched millions of dollars get out from behind the wheel.

Jonah Green was not exactly a typical patron of the Log Cabin. At least sixty, he had a commanding presence, even from a distance, six foot one and perhaps two-hundred-twenty pounds with only a slight paunch and a close-cropped, almost military haircut that minimized both the gray and the receding hairline. His face was square, including his jaw, and grooved with lessons learned and given.

From my perch I couldn't see his eyes, but they were searching the landscape and, for one unnerving moment, his gaze seemed to linger on me, even though he couldn't be seeing me, not without his own binoculars.

I lowered mine. "Your father."

"No shit!"

"He's early—a good hour."

"So are you."

I raised them. "I'm a lying untrustworthy shit."

"…Good to know."

From a pocket of his topcoat—dark gray and probably Saville Row, unbuttoned and providing a glimpse of a well-tailored gray suit over Italian loafers—he withdrew something. I couldn't tell for sure, but it seemed to be a cell phone.

He spoke into it, briefly.

The object was returned to the topcoat pocket, and Green stood there inhaling deeply and exhaling smoky breath until, within a minute, a second car pulled in, a nondescript number, a brown Taurus.

This gave me a momentary start, because the car was similar if not identical to the rental Harry Something had driven, an automobile I had yet to deal with (it would need disposal, probably in one of the gravel pits intended for Julie, before I came along).

But this turned out to be a coincidence—and how I hate those—when its driver got out, a brawny dipshit in a brand-new green-and-black hunting jacket and matching flop-ear Elmer Fudd cap. In his early twenties, this ripe specimen had broad shoulders and close-set eyes in an oval face that seemed utterly blank from this distance. I had a hunch a closer look wouldn't fill that oval in much.

The two men began to speak, though Green did most of the talking, gesturing, giving orders. At the start of this one-sided exchange, Green's flunky took off the Fudd cap respectfully, revealing blond hair, cut even shorter than his boss's; he would nod when it seemed appropriate.

I centered on their faces, and I had a good three-quarter angle on Jonah Green, with a decent side view of his boy. Much of what I have done over the years involves surveillance, and while I never studied the art, I'd picked up lip-reading early on.

Green was saying, "Prick'll probably show early. Stay sharp."

"How will I recognize him?"

"Oh, I don't know—maybe because he has my *daughter* with him?"

The subordinate blushed. I'm not lying. He fucking blushed, and shook his head and said, "Right. Right! Sorry. That was dumb. Really dumb."

The millionaire just looked at him, for the longest time, then said, "Form the thought. Examine it. Decide if it's worth sharing. Understand this concept, De-something?"

Green didn't say "De-something," obviously; I just hadn't gotten the name—DeWitt maybe?

Whatever his handle, the Fudd-hatted fool nodded, his eyes lowered, ashamed. "Yes, sir."

Then his disgusted boss, with a dismissive gesture toward his subordinate's brown rental, headed inside the restaurant, and the doofus got in the Taurus and drove it over and parked in the graveled overflow lot, turning the engine off but not emerging.

Keeping watch.

I lowered the binoculars again. "Your daddy's not alone—young guy. Blond. Body builder."

"That would be DeWayne."

"DeWayne."

She shrugged, not giving a shit. "He was some kind of…I don't know, super soldier."

I looked at her. "Really."

She shrugged again. "Cleans things up for Daddy, these days."

"…Too young for Desert Storm."

"Iraq."

That made me smile, and she said, "What's so funny?"

"Nothing," I said.

An hour went by, during which the girl said she had to pee, twice, and I ignored it the first time and the second time said, "Hold it. You can use the restaurant's john."

"*When?*" Her teeth were chattering again. "How

much longer are you going to keep my daddy waiting like this?"

"Not much."

I'd spotted Green in a window, seated in a booth within the restaurant, and right now he and DeWayne were having a cell phone conversation, a little heated on Green's part. No lip-reading was possible, but I got the gist—*where the fuck was I?*

I put the binoculars in my left jacket pocket, and stuck my right hand in the other pocket for the nine millimeter which I then stuffed in my waistband, and said to her, "Time for Daddy and pissing," and she said, "Aren't I the lucky one," and I hauled her up off the snowy ground by the elbow.

"What's the plan?" she asked, as I led her through the woods.

But I didn't answer her till we'd crossed the highway, a good half-mile down from the Log Cabin, when we were in the wooded area, heading back around behind the restaurant.

"The plan," I said, "is you behave yourself and I don't kill your pretty ass."

"I didn't know you cared."

When we entered through the kitchen, the girl's handcuffed hands were still under my draped-over loaner jacket, and I had to give her credit, she didn't cause any trouble or indicate anything was wrong.

The short-order cook, an olive-skinned guy who

might have been Greek or Turkish or some shit, didn't understand English; but he got the drift of a ten-spot quick enough, and—when I gestured toward the dining area—let us pass without incident.

We stopped at the ladies' room ("Setters")—a single seater, but there was room enough in there for both of us.

"What are you—kinky?" she asked, as she undid her jeans.

"No," I said. "Careful."

She sat. "You *could* turn your back."

"Girls with nipple rings don't get to be shy and retiring."

"Fuck you," she said over the noise she was making.

"I already passed—remember?"

She smirked, wiped herself, stood, pulled up her drawers; her pussy was shaved, and I caught a glint of another ring down there—why was I not surprised?

But punkette or not, she took time to wash her hands, dainty little thing that she was. I gave her plenty of room, not caring to have her toss soapy water in my eyes.

As we emerged, a middle-aged woman in a kitty sweater was waiting and she gave us a look.

"You don't want to know," I advised her, and she seemed to agree, slipping inside the little ladies room. The gulf between shaved pussy and kitty sweaters is a wide one.

The folksy, hunting-themed restaurant had filled up some, farmers, truck drivers, assorted locals— half the booths taken, most of the stools at the counter, too.

Sticking out like a well-tailored sore thumb, Jonah Green—still in his Saville Row topcoat in his window booth—half-rose when he spotted us coming from behind the counter toward him. He glanced ever so slightly, frowningly, toward the window—out where DeWayne was sitting guard, not missing anything, remember?—and Julie and I slid in opposite him.

"Mr. Green," I said, with a nod.

He formed a tiny sneer large with contempt; his eyes, like his car, were money color. "And what shall I call you? Besides forty-two fucking minutes late."

"Quarry."

"What kind of name is that?"

"A false one." I glanced at Julie. "You seem over-joyed to see your daughter, alive and well."

Prompted, he leaned forward and sent his eyes to her. "Are you all right, Julie?"

"Fuck you," she said.

Her list of responses was limited, but got the job done.

Her father sighed and looked at me as if seeking support or sympathy or something the fuck he wasn't going to get.

He asked, "Do you have any children, Mr. Quarry?"

"Besides your daughter? No."

He shook his head. "I fly through the goddamn night in a goddamn private jet to deliver this goddamn money, and *this*…"

"Mr. Green," I interrupted tightly. "Some discretion, please?"

"…is the *thanks* I get. The appreciation." Another sigh, a world-weary shrug. "But that's the modern world, isn't it, Mr. Quarry? Values. They're nonexistent these days, aren't they?"

I shifted in the booth. "You really don't want to stall me, Mr. Green. Your daughter will tell you how little compunction I have about making people who annoy me go away."

He studied me for perhaps five seconds—it seemed longer; and he smiled a little, as he did, which would have been unnerving if I impressed easily.

"An intelligent man," Green said softly. "Possibly educated."

"Flattery is probably not the approach you want to take, Mr. Green."

"…How did you happen to, uh…intercept my daughter from those people?"

I shook my head. "That information is not included in the purchase price—shall we get on with business?"

His eyes tightened and he nodded. "Yes. Why don't we?…And let me assure you, sir, that's how I view this transaction—strictly business."

Julie said, "Jesus Christ—now I'm a transaction. Can I get some fucking apple pie or something?"

Her long-suffering parent closed his eyes.

"Charm school didn't take?" I asked him.

The millionaire flagged down a waitress, and said, "Apple pie for my daughter, please. And coffee. She likes it black."

The waitress, a redhead who'd been beautiful fifteen years ago, scribbled, then looked at me over her pad. "Anything for you, honey?"

"No. Thanks."

She disappeared.

Julie was sitting forward and grinning nastily at her old man. "Wow—I'm blown the fuck away!" Then she looked at me. "Son of a bitch knows how I like my *coffee!*" And back at him: "How old am I, Jonah? What's my *boyfriend's* name?"

Her father gave her an expression as blank as brick. "You don't *have* a boyfriend, not since I paid Martin Luther Van Dross to take a hike. He loved you a whole ten grand worth, angel. So, yes, I *know* you like it black."

"You bastard," she said, and her eyes were tearing. "You heartless fucking bastard...."

I said, "This is touching, and would make great reality TV; but if you two don't mind—business?"

Julie glared out the window.

Green shifted his weight, his eyes unblinking but

not exactly cold as they settled on me. "I just want you to know, Mr. Quarry, that there will be no efforts made against you. Not with the law, not privately— and a man with my resources could easily do that, either way. But you saved my daughter's life…and I value that. I do value that."

Julie's jaw tightened but her eyes didn't leave the window.

"Swell," I said. "I value money. Where is it?"

Green lifted an eyebrow, offered up a half-smile that was wholly conspiratorial. "If you'll reach under the table…I trust you prefer that I not reach under there myself…you will find a briefcase."

My left hand found it easily. I hauled the brown-leather attache up beside me, near the aisle, away from the girl.

I said, "I'd be annoyed if this contained pepper spray or dye or some such shit."

"I'm sure you would be," Green said, reasonably. "But you'll find it's all there—just as you asked.…" He lowered his voice to a whisper. "Small bills. Unmarked."

"Is this case locked?"

"No."

"Well, your daughter's handcuffs are," I said, a foot in the aisle. "I'm going to the men's room to count this. I'll be back with the cuff key."

Julie, eyes finally leaving the window, chimed in:

"Good. That way I won't have to stick my face in my pie....Mr. Quarry here *loves* it when I talk dirty, Daddy."

Green ignored her, saying to me, "You really trust me, trust *us*, to be here when you get back?"

All sarcasm and attitude gone, serious as a heart attack, Julie leaned forward and gave her father the following advice: "Don't *fuck* with this guy, Daddy...."

The magnate lost his cool momentarily: "Why— didn't *you*?"

Her upper lip peeled back over teeth as white as they were feral: "No...but not for lack of trying."

Green heaved his largest sigh yet, gathered his dignity and said to me, "You'll have to forgive our little family bickering, Mr. Quarry, but—"

"If this isn't money," I told him, hefting the briefcase, already half out of the booth, "I'll find you in hell."

Green summoned another half-smile but his eyes were narrow. "Isn't that a little melodramatic, coming from you, Mr. Quarry?"

"Yeah," I admitted. "But from what I see, melodrama is what you people understand....If you'll excuse me."

I could feel the millionaire's eyes on my back as I headed to the men's room, passing the redheaded waitress bearing Julie's pie and coffee as I did.

And before I took the turn toward the restrooms, I could hear the handcuffed girl blurt, "Ah shit," behind me. Maybe she'd have to stick her face in that pie, after all.

The men's room ("Pointers") was another small single-stool affair, but I knew that. I was not a regular here by any means, having only stopped at the Log Cabin twice since coming to the area; but I remembered the window, and the briefcase and I went out it.

DeWayne was behind the wheel, keeping loyal if pointless watch when I slipped in on the passenger side, the briefcase handle in my left hand and the nine millimeter in my right.

The gun was low, in my lap, as I pointed it up at the oval, unformed face.

His eyes were light blue and wide as hell when he looked at me, and then down into the dark unfathomable eye of the automatic's snout.

"Fuck a duck," he said.

His voice was on the high side, about a second tenor; but at least he didn't squeak.

I asked him, "Are you going to make me kill you, DeWayne?"

His eyelashes, which were long and oddly feminine, fluttered. "No. Hell no!"

He put his hands up, shoulder high.

"Put those down," I told him.

He did.

He seemed a little hurt—here he'd been trying to cooperate and voluntarily raised his hands, and all he got for it was a sharp rebuke. It's a tough world, DeWayne.

I gestured with the nine. "Now put your weapon and your cell phone, pager, keys, anything in your pockets, on the seat here between us."

DeWayne carried that out—his gun was a glock—and he was about done when I asked, "What branch?"

He frowned, parsing that, then said, "Marines."

That got a dry chuckle out of me. "Semper fi, Mac."

This caused DeWayne to brighten with hope. "You, too...? Where'd you serve?"

"In a real war....Now get out and open the trunk."

He swallowed, nodded, and within seconds he was crawling up inside the Taurus trunk, a big ungainly fetus making a tight fit. The overflow lot was empty, except for us, and the windows on this end of the restaurant were vacant. So we were cool.

His expression was pitiful when he said, "Thanks."

"What for?"

"Not...not killing me."

"It's early yet," I said.

And slammed the trunk shut.

Super soldier.

Jonah Green's face was in his booth's window when I pulled out casually in DeWayne's rental vehicle. Julie Green's face was in the window, too. She was laughing her ass off.

"*Goddamnit!*" her father yelled.

Didn't take a seasoned lip-reader to make that out.

Five

And that should have been the end of it.

I'd left DeWayne in the trunk of his rental at the rest stop where my Jag waited. The kid's glock and belongings I left in the front seat—no call to take them and, anyway, I'm not a fucking thief.

I'd cleaned up after myself, disposing of Harry's brown Taurus in the gravel pit, and doing further clean-up at the cottage, and put the money in a safe deposit box at Brainerd.

Rationalization is a seductive bitch, and I'd pretty much convinced myself that if Harry and Louis turned into floaters on that lake after the thaw, their mob credentials would get the killings written off as Chicago fun and games.

Almost a month had passed when, on an afternoon so overcast that the northwoods were more blue and gray than green and brown, I was lounging in the hot tub in the barnwood-sided building that housed my personal off-season sauna and swimming pool. The world outside was cold as fuck, but my indoors universe was pleasantly muggy, the jet streams working on that chronic low back of mine like Spanish dancers minus the castanets.

I didn't even have trunks on. Since I was the sole winter resident of Sylvan Lodge, except on the two days a week José came around, I would just jog across the private lane to the pool building without even my jacket, and go in and strip down and swim a few laps, sauna a while and wind up in the Jacuzzi. I liked the free feeling, but in retrospect, bare-ass was vulnerable.

And vulnerable is not a condition I like to put myself in.

I was nursing a can of Diet Coke, the tub's jets feeling just fine, and the events of less than a month ago were nowhere in my mind. Even over the hot tub burble, I heard the sound of the glass doors opening—this was *not* one of José's days—and my hand drifted toward my folded towel, under which was the nine millimeter.

Bare-ass is one thing; unarmed something else again....

Jonah Green appeared to be alone.

I could see another Lexus parked out front—this one sky-blue—and no driver was apparent. The millionaire was in a jogging suit the color of his name with running shoes and no jacket or topcoat, despite the cold; and his face was red with the weather because of it.

My first instinct was, he wanted me to know (or anyway think) he was not armed.

Very tentatively, he stood there with a glass door slid open, halfway in, and—with a deference I didn't figure was usual coming from this man—asked, "May I come in?"

I just looked at him.

When he didn't get permission, he came in just the same, closing the door behind him, and was goddamn lucky he wasn't dead by the time he turned and said, "Don't get your balls in an uproar, Mr. Quarry—I'm alone."

Deference hadn't worked, so he'd gone straight to hard-nosed.

He was moving cautiously my way, saying, "And if you kill me, you won't know how I found you."

I said nothing.

He nodded, as if I'd actually answered, then came over and pulled up a metal deck chair and sat at the edge of the Jacuzzi, nearby but not getting in my space.

"Don't worry," he said, patting the steamy air. His expression was soft, the grooves in his face at ease; but the money-color eyes were hard. "I didn't waste my resources finding you to get...*even*, or some idiotic bullshit."

I said nothing.

Sitting forward slightly in the chair, Green said, "Before you kill me—strangle me with that towel or whatever, I would—"

I showed him the nine millimeter from under the towel.

"There's an elegant expression," he said with admirable cool. " 'Don't shit where you eat'....You live here, you manage this place, you have a *life*... why risk that with a death?...Hear me out."

I said nothing, but I lowered the gun a fraction.

He put his hands on his chest. "I really do appreciate what you did for me, and my daughter. I'm well aware that those mob fagellehs would've killed the little smartass."

I said, "Our business is over."

He shrugged, a tiny smile forming, pleased he'd finally drawn me out into at least speaking. "Our *old* business is over, Mr. Quarry—I really do admire your resourcefulness, your abilities. Take DeWayne, for example."

"No thanks."

He shrugged in an admission of his subordinate's imperfection. "DeWayne isn't brilliant, but he's dangerous. You handled him as if he were a helpless child."

"A couple thousand DeWaynes have died in Iraq."

The millionaire sighed, nodded, slumping in his metal chair. He shook his head. "And a goddamned shame."

I shrugged with one shoulder. "We spilled more than that."

Picking up on my attitude, and instantly getting over his sorrow for the lost lives in Iraq, Jonah Green said, "I'm sure you did. Which is why I won't make the mistake of sending a boy to do a man's work again....I've asked around about you, Mr. Quarry. By the way, is that a first name or a last name?"

"Probably."

That stopped him for a beat, then he moved on briskly, almost cheerfully. "At any rate, I did some asking around....I do business in all kinds of circles, you know."

"You talk in circles, too. What do you want, Mr. Green?"

He semi-ignored that question. "Seems there's a certain freelance assassin who dropped out of sight, a few years ago. He had a reputation as the best man in a tough game, sort of a killer's killer. He wasn't mob, although sometimes he did jobs for—"

"I'm impressed you found me. Trouble is, now I have to move."

I raised the gun.

Finally he got it, or maybe my raising the nine just let out the nervousness that had been inside him all along. His hands flew up, as if this were a stick-up.

He was half a second away from dead when he blurted, "I want you to do a job for me! Another job!"

My finger froze on the trigger.

This was a lot of money seated near me, begging me to let him give me some. I'm not a greedy man; but I'm not a monk, either.

I said, "I'm retired."

He knew he'd made a dent and something lively came into the green eyes. "That would've been just before the stock market went to shit, wouldn't it? How are your investments doing, Mr. Quarry? Did you get out before the dotcom bust?"

"I'm comfortable," I said, which was funny in a way, because I was naked in a hot tub, so of course I was comfortable. On the other hand, I was holding a nine millimeter, thinking about killing this prick; so that part wasn't so comfortable.

"So comfortable," he said, unintentionally mirroring my thoughts in an openly Faustian manner, "that you wouldn't come out of retirement for a quarter of a million dollars?"

Again I lowered the gun a hair. "…It's not a political job, is it?"

"No! No, no, no."

I sighed again, this time for my own benefit. "One last job is always a bad idea. Guys die trying to retire on one last job all the time."

"But you are not just *any* guy, are you, Mr. Quarry?" He smiled; he had the same white feral teeth as his daughter, only his might have been false. The teeth part. The feral was real.

"No," I admitted, "I'm not. What makes it worth a quarter mil?"

He answered with another question: "Do you have any reservations about taking out a woman?"

"I take women out all the time."

"Not the way *I* mean."

I smiled just a little. "Are you sure?"

We sat in my kitchen.

Jonah Green already knew the lay of my land, so there was no harm in taking him across the road to the A-frame cottage…no further harm, anyway. Plus, I was tired of negotiating with my dick hanging out. Water's a bad place to hold a serious conversation, at least your half of it; the other guy can always make his point by kicking something electrical in—I know, because I've been that guy.

So now we were both dressed. The Mr. Coffee was on, and we were exploring the job. The only step remaining was me deciding to do the thing or not—the money required no further discussion.

A captain of industry through and through, Jonah Green had a folder of information, including half a dozen photos. The woman in the photos—all candid, surveillance-type—was in her early thirties, attractive but not making the most of it, her hair up, with reading glasses on in some of the shots.

She did not look like a likely contract-murder

victim, but you never know. Karen Silkwood didn't look like much, either (no, I didn't do that one).

He was handing me across several information-crammed sheets. "Here's everything you need to know about the woman—work and home addresses, personal habits and friends, everything."

I glanced up at him. "Time frame?"

Green blinked. "Say again? I don't follow."

"You need her dead—I get that. *When* do you need her dead?"

He sat forward; for the first time the talk took on a truly conspiratorial feel. "In two months, her being alive is…a bad thing for me." He sighed, and something that might have been regret, real or feigned, came into his expression and his voice. "Understand, Mr. Quarry, she didn't do anything to deserve—"

I cut him off with a traffic-cop palm. "Mr. Green…you're a powerful guy. You've decided you need her dead. That means she's already dead."

His forehead and eyes tightened. "I…now I really don't follow…."

Tossing the pictures on the table, I said, "She's already dead—she just doesn't know it yet. My doing the job is…a detail."

That made the millionaire slightly ill at ease, and he said, maybe for his own peace of mind, "Well, it's strictly a matter of business—nothing personal. She's a nice woman, I'm sure—"

"Nice women," I interrupted, "don't make themselves the targets of men like you, who aren't nice."

Blood drained from his face, but he said nothing. Hard to get indignant when the guy you're hiring to kill somebody points out that you're not Mr. Wonderful.

I gestured with the information sheets.

"This stuff is fine," I said. "But understand, Mr. Green, I have to watch her a while, anyway. A few days, at least."

He frowned, shaking his head, pointing to the info sheets. "But…I've got all her patterns recorded, already…library…apartment.…"

"How old is the information? A P.I. gathered this. When?"

The frown deepened into irritation, as if I had questioned his professionalism. "I tell you, it's fresh!"

"*How* fresh?"

Now he sounded defensive, and did a Rodney Dangerfield tug of his jogging-suit collar. "A month, six weeks at the outside."

I shook my head. "I have to watch her a while. Patterns change. Shift." I sat forward. "Mr. Green, the elimination side is only part of the process—it starts with surveillance. Otherwise the cops find me. And if they find me, they find you."

In the old days, the guy hiring me wouldn't have

been sitting across from me; it would have been the Broker or someone like him.

Jonah Green let out a sigh worthy of a Christian martyr. "Fine." His eyebrows rose and he shook a finger. "But *two months*, and she's a problem, Mr. Quarry."

"I heard that the first time."

He tasted the inside of his mouth and didn't seem to like it much. "There's, uh…one other thing. It's a part of why your fee is so generous."

"Let's hear it."

"It's…well, it's got to be an accident."

I didn't like the sound of that. "Say again?"

He gestured with both hands, obviously finding it distasteful to have to discuss this. "You know…slip and fall in the tub, brakes go out, hell, *I* don't know… that's *your* department!"

I looked at him for a while.

He was getting uneasy by the time I said, "I don't usually do 'accidents.' "

Irritably, he said, "For a quarter mil, make an exception—you mind if I smoke?"

"Take it outside."

Dusk had settled on us as we stood on the deck, looking out on Sylvan Lake's still frozen expanse; you couldn't see Harry and Louis's hole at all from here.

The millionaire leaned on the deck rail, gazing out

at the stark, serene landscape, his plumes of breath alternating with exhales of tobacco smoke. I was standing there, arms folded, looking at my prospective employer, wondering if I should take the job or go out there and drop another one in that hole.

"Beautiful," Green said, shaking his head admiringly. "Beautiful goddamn country, up here. I can see why you like it."

"I'll be moving on soon," I said. "You could probably buy this cottage from the guy who owns the lodge."

Green flicked his gaze my way.

I continued: "Of course, if you do move in, for a summer home? Every time you look out at this lovely lake, you'll be looking at those numbnuts who grabbed your kid."

He wasn't studying the lake, anymore; his eyes were on me. "Why moving on?"

"You know where I live, Mr. Green." I shrugged and smiled. "Even if I *do* do this job, I'm out of here."

Eyes narrowed to slits, Green said, "You don't need to do that, Mr. Quarry. I swear to you I was discreet about finding you. I used a number of people, and no single investigator was—"

"Sure. Fine."

Green sighed. "*Will* you do the job?"

I nodded.

Relief flooded his features. "How do I make my payment?"

"I'll give you the offshore banking info. When $125K hits the account, I go to work. When I deliver, put the rest in."

Green frowned. "You trust me to do that?"

"Sure." I grinned at him. "I'm kinda my own collection agency."

He didn't allow himself to be frightened by that; instead he again stared out at the hauntingly beautiful lake.

For the first time, I heard a genuine melancholy in the mogul's voice. "She's...she's *already* dead."

I nodded. "It just hasn't made the obits yet.... Coffee?"

Six

The Homewood Library seemed modern to me, but only because of my age—it dated to the '70s and you walked into a big high-ceilinged area with wide steps leading up to a surrounding second floor that was like a landing that got out of hand.

The place was all cheerful oranges and greens and yellows, dotted with oppressively cheerful posters encouraging reading and featuring lots of Asian and black faces, though everybody I saw in there was white. What had once been open and spacious was now a little cluttered, with an area obviously intended for seating given over to portable bookcases of NEW RELEASES and AUDIOS, and various computer stations.

It didn't remind me much of the austere church-like libraries of my youth—hardwood floors and institutional green walls and endless shelves of anonymous dustjacket-less books overseen by cold-eyed old-maid librarians with their hair in gray buns and their bodies in gray dresses that a nun would've considered needlessly unflattering.

And Janet Wright didn't remind me of those old-maid librarians, either, though her white blouse and black skirt were a little stark, at that. Her dark blonde hair was pinned up (though not in a bun), attractive stray curls of it struggling free to give her heart-shaped face unbidden decorative touches. Her reading glasses were wireframe and merely serviceable, like the touches of lipstick and eyeliner that appeared to be her only makeup. She seemed to have a nice shape, too, though her wardrobe played it down.

But there was no getting away from that nice, creamy complexion and eyes so brown they almost looked black from a distance, and she had a very nice smile that she flashed generously at the grade-school kids—third-graders?—who were sitting on the floor in the Children's Section staring up adoringly at her, lost in the story she was reading...a book called *The Glass Doorknob*, something or other about a sock monkey.

I was impressed—not one of these kids was fidgeting or squirming or looking to need their Ritalin dosage, even if their laughter did seem unnecessarily shrill. Of course, eight kids who were spending their Friday after-school time at the library probably weren't the type to be fussy; plus, the six girls probably wanted to be Janet Wright when they grew up, and the two boys probably wanted to marry her when they did (although right now they had no idea why).

As she sat in the chair, her audience gathered

around like little Indians, it was obvious she related well to the tykes, stopping to ask them questions, involving them, really looking at them and even listening to their answers.

Already I understood what Jonah Green had meant about this woman not deserving what I was here to do to her. Nobody looking at her would have guessed a contract kill would be her fate. On the other hand, nobody looking at me would have guessed I was stalking my prey—in jeans, running shoes, brown sweater, lighter brown shirt-with-collar, I might have been a teacher or writer, the kind of rumpled jerk who browses endlessly at Borders and never buys a goddamn thing, then complains that book sales are down because the world has gone illiterate.

Right now I was fucking around in the War Section, flipping through books on Vietnam written by idiots who hadn't been there. And, by the way, if you ever have a question about where any specific subjects can be found in the stacks of the Homewood Library, from gardening to the Holocaust, I'm your guy.

She'd been easy enough to spot—from the handful of pictures Green had given me, plus when I came in she was sitting at the HELP DESK with her name on a nameplate in front of her. It didn't take Sherlock Holmes or Miss Marple to make her.

She also worked the front desk, during lunch hour, checking out books, pleasant, friendly, helpful to various library patrons, clearly good at what she did and happy doing it.

I kept browsing, "reading" magazines and books while I kept up my surveillance, lately keeping track of Janet Wright interacting with these laughing children. It was the kind of thing that would give you a warm feeling if you weren't here to kill her.

After the kids scampered off to their suppers, Janet returned to the help desk where she was doing paperwork when a narrow-faced, conventionally handsome guy approached her, a thirty-something would-be Yuppie with a tan, perfect hair, a pale yellow shirt with an alligator on it and jeans that were too new-looking.

I was nearby, pretty much directly behind my subject, going through old bound volumes of *Life* magazine from the '40s and '50s, stopping at the surprisingly frequent shots of starlets in bathing suits.

A conversation started up between my librarian and the Yuppie, for which lip-reading would not have been a necessary step—in fact, the obnoxious Yuppie made it hard not to overhear. Apparently this whole quiet-it's-a-library concept was foreign to him.

He flicked the HELP DESK sign and said, with a grin that told me he appreciated his own wit, "I could use some help."

The librarian I could barely make out, and her back was to me.

But I think she said, "Rick—please. Not here."

He leaned a palm against the edge of the desk and his smile was a white slash in the too-tanned face.

"Come on—you're not still *mad*...."

She said nothing, her head down. She was doing paperwork, or pretending to.

The smile disappeared and he leaned in, his expression approximating humility. "Baby. Come on. I didn't mean anything by it."

On her response, I heard her just fine: she wasn't talking any louder, but the words were crisp and clear.

"Next time," she said, looking right up at him, "I'll call nine-one-one. I swear I will."

He drew back; shrugged. "Hey. You pissed me off. Deal with it."

She slammed a book shut.

"I *am* dealing with it," she said.

"Baby..."

"You had no right—no right."

And now she looked back down at her work.

"It's over, Rick," she said. "Don't make me call security."

He leaned in again, got another smile going, though it bordered on a sneer. "Why—you want another scene?" He laughed and it sounded forced. "Sometimes I think you *like* scenes."

She said nothing. Did not look up at him.

He turned to go, but had only moved a step when he looked back and said, "Hey—pick you up. Usual time."

"No. No!"

"Meet you, then."

He shot her a goodbye with a gun of thumb-and-forefinger, and sauntered off, cocky as hell. She didn't bother to reply.

Pity—seems like nobody ever hires you to kill a prick like that.

Another librarian, a busty, almost plump woman also in her early thirties, moved in and pulled up a chair-on-wheels from somewhere and sat behind the desk with Janet. The second librarian had on a bright pink blouse and darker pink slacks; her hair was very blonde and big and sprayed, and her makeup was loud. Fuckable, though.

"Janet," she was saying, making no attempt to keep her voice down, "you have *got* to do something about that *creep!*"

Janet shrugged. "I told him it's over, Connie. I told him just now."

"Do you think he *heard* you? You think he ever really listens to *anything* you say? Listen to me, sweetie. He is going to *really* hurt you, next time."

Janet, who had swiveled on her own wheeled chair, to face her colleague, sighed and shook her head. "Maybe....maybe he's right. Maybe it was my fault."

"*Your* fault?"

She was shaking her head. "I shouldn't've made him mad. I mean, I knew about his temper. When you touch a hot stove and get burned, you can't blame the—"

Connie put her hand over Janet's mouth and leaned in closer.

"Talk like that," she said, "and *I'll* send you to the emergency room."

Then Connie withdrew her hand from Janet's mouth and cupped her friend's chin with that same hand and leaned in close. I had to lip-read now, but I got it. Probably I'd have got it just from the busty one's compassionate expression and the other's cha-grined one.

"Do you hear what I'm saying, Janet?"

"I do. I do. I'm not seeing him anymore."

"And if he hurts you—the police?"

A laugh that wasn't a laugh. "What good would that do, in this town?"

Connie's features were stone. "They have to write it up. And you can see a lawyer if you need to. There are ways to deal with jerks like Rick."

She was right about that.

Connie said, "Word to the wise," and shook a

mildly scolding finger, got up, and moved away, guiding the wheeled chair back to wherever the hell she got it.

A few moments later, Janet left the help desk and I followed her, a half room of shelved books between us, me seeing her flickeringly as I moved along, strobe style. Or maybe I was just getting punchy spending all this time around so many books.

Finally she stopped at a water fountain.

Nervously, she put something in her mouth— a pill?

She bent at the fountain and, when she pressed the handle to create an arc of water, her sleeve rode up a little, and revealed part of a purple bruise.

I shook my head.

Rick might have been somehow important or connected in this town (as the busty librarian had indicated), but that didn't make him any less a brutal dunce. Takes a lot of awful people to make up this old world.

From another conversation Janet and Connie had, I got the drift that my target's work day was drawing to a close, so I gathered my jacket from a chair at a reading table and headed outside into the cold, clean—if thin—mountain air.

Homewood reminded me a little of Boulder, Colorado, minus the heavy tourism. Thirty thousand or so had the privilege of living in this idyllic little burg, where mountains edged a sky so blue, clouds should've paid rent for the privilege. I felt lucky to have a contract take me to such pleasant if dull surroundings; it helped make up for having to kill somebody as harmless as Janet Wright seemed to be.

Dusk was settling when Janet emerged from the library with her friend Connie and another librarian, whose name was Don, my surveillance had gathered. A nerd.

From my rental vehicle—a blue Taurus (was that all these fucking rental agencies had these days?)—I watched as the librarians paused to chat and then go their separate ways.

Janet's vehicle was parked on the street—I'd observed her going out and feeding the meter every two hours, during the six I spent in the library. She got into the little yellow Geo, mid-'90s vintage, started it up and pulled away, moving right across my line of vision.

Her rear bumper had stickers that I could have predicted—she was still advertising KERRY/EDWARDS 2004, among other lost leftist causes—and started my own car and took off after her, in slow pursuit.

I followed her, usually with a few cars between us, through sleepy Homewood, from the downtown and on through a quietly affluent residential section; it was the kind of place Norman Rockwell could have painted, though had he spent much more than an afternoon here, he might have hanged himself out of boredom.

Soon the town had disappeared, as had my cover traffic, and she was out into the countryside, making my job harder.

Already my point was proven about the staleness of my client's research: Janet Wright was not headed in the direction of her own apartment, the address for which was the first place I'd checked out getting to town. Nor was there anything in the written reports indicating that anything out this way was a regular stop of hers.

When Janet Wright turned down a lane into a deeply wooded area, I almost missed it; then I caught the tail of her Geo between the trees, and drove on. Pulled into a driveway half a mile later, turned around, and followed.

In five minutes, I caught sight of her pulling off the lane into a private drive. Cutting my speed to almost nothing, I waited until she was well out of view, then moved on by, and parked alongside the road, what there was of it. I walked back and slipped into the trees along the private drive; the snow on the ground was minimal, my shoes crunching on leaves and twigs underneath the dusting, and I was in no danger of earning my Inconspicuous Tracker Merit

Badge. But I didn't worry about that—I could see her getting out of her Geo, fiddling for her keys in her purse, clearly oblivious to my presence.

Still, my hand was on the nine millimeter in my jacket pocket. You never knew.

The Geo was parked in front of a secluded, expensive, sprawling home, not quite a mansion but oozing money, modern in the Frank Lloyd Wright manner, a story and a half with lots of wood and stone blending in nicely with the surrounding naturescape.

At the front door, she stooped on the stoop to pick up a newspaper, then gathered mail from the mailbox.

I was closer to the house now, and watched through a side window as she entered, mail and paper bundled in one arm, entering via a key in her other hand, pushing the door open—it was a little stubborn. A security tone kicked in, and a dog began to bark…from the sound of it, a small one, lapdog likely.

Which was good. A pinscher or a pit bull can ruin your day.

Janet went to a touchpad by the door and entered a code. I had an angle through the window that showed me her fingertips doing it, and I committed the numbers to memory, even if I did have to move my lips.

At a table near the door, already piled with rolled-up newspapers and stacked magazines and envelopes, the librarian stood and sorted through the mail, putting individual items into their respective piles. Throughout, two things were a constant: I watched; and the dog barked.

She spoke to one of us, in a loud firm voice: "Just a sec, Poochie! Gimme a sec."

Housesitting, most likely.

Through a kitchen window I watched as she unpenned the small dog—a little black-and-white rat terrier—who danced and yapped and danced and yapped for Janet. She knelt and petted it and it stood on its hind legs and lapped her face and whimpered orgiastically. About thirty seconds of good-girl-good-doggie talk followed. This I did not commit to memory.

I'd missed it, but while she was down there, Janet had attached a small leash to the dog, and when she and the doggie headed toward the back door, near the window I was peeking through, I damn near blew it.

But I got behind a tree in time, and then she was walking the terrier in the expansive, unfenced back yard, being careful not to walk in spots where the pooch had already made a deposit.

Over the next fifteen minutes, I kept watch as the

woman and dog returned inside, and the woman put water and food down for the dog, re-penned it, then went around the house, watering plants.

Housesitting, for sure.

She was in the dining room when she finished the watering, and that's where and when she began unbuttoning her blouse.

I kept watching as the blouse came open and a pinkish excuse for a bra was revealed; then the blouse and bra came off and nice breasts were revealed. Though she was in her thirties, no sag at all was apparent, full almost-C cups with half-dollar-size areolae and nipples that extended perhaps a half inch, soft.

She dropped the blouse and the bra to the floor, casually, and walked back into the kitchen, topless. There she stepped out of her skirt and revealed a half slip, which she also shed, letting me in on one of Victoria's best secrets: lacy-edged pink panties cut high on the hip. Then she stepped out of those, as graceful as a dancer but so much more natural, moving on, leaving the clothes behind, littering lingerie. Her ass didn't sag, either, her back beautifully dimpled above the firm roundness.

I paused for a moment. Shadowing this woman to fill a contract was one thing; but watching her disrobe seemed wrong, somehow.

Still, surveillance was surveillance....

Taking to the trees again, I scurried around the house, tripping on a root but not quite falling, and found my way to the rear of the place, where glass doors looked in on a swimming pool room, fairly elaborate, about two-thirds the size of the similar area back at Sylvan Lodge, and similar faux-rustic.

I positioned myself where I could see her as she entered—she was nude now, and wholly at ease, because how could she know some asshole was watching her, getting a hard-on?

But who could blame my dick for getting stiff? This was a nice-looking woman. No shaved pussy for my librarian, this was a full, old-fashioned bush, maybe trimmed back just a little, dark blonde and a nice contrast to her pale, creamy flesh. She had a classic shape, five foot five with a rib cage providing a nice display area for the perky rack, waist wasping in, hips flaring out. Her legs were a little heavy by today's standards, but fuck today's standards.

This was a woman.

A woman who walked to the deep end and dove in.

Which to witness, I don't mind telling you, was in its way thrilling.

So I watched her swim. I watched her swim for a long time, taking her relaxation at the end of her working day by stroking the water, smoothly graceful, and then on her back, a dreamily sensuous if unintentional performance, and why wouldn't it be?

She was nude, and she was beautiful.

And so I did my job, keeping her under surveillance, and my dick throbbed in my pants. Which is where I left it. I wasn't going to unzip and jerk off or anything.

Jesus.

What kind of guy do you think I am?

Seven

Pushing the southern outskirts of Homewood, Sneaky Pete's was one of those slightly upscale country-western bars where shitkickers were not welcome but young professionals were. In the low-slung brick building's barely lighted parking lot—asphalt not gravel—you'd be more likely to see a Navigator than a Ford F150. Once inside, the music was that painfully homogenized country pop of the Faith Hill and Brooks and Dunn variety; the only saving grace was line dancing having gone out of fashion.

This was just your typical middle-class/upper-middle-class meat market, and a guy in his fifties had to work to look inconspicuous among all these twenty- and thirty-somethings.

It helped that the place was packed—this was Friday night, and lively with laughter, clinking glasses, and the promise of hooking up. Even though I was not a smoker, the notion that a bar like this was A SMOKE-FREE ENVIRONMENT seemed wrong, even wacky. Would entire generations of Americans grow up going out Friday and Saturday nights, not coming home with their bodies and clothing reeking of smoke? Another communal experience lost....

I was not able to sit as near Janet and her friend Connie as I would have liked. They were in a booth to my back, with a cluster of tables between us. But I was facing a bar with a mirrored wall, and my lip-reading skills came in handy.

The conversation I am about to report I admit took some filling in with my imagination, when my vision was blocked by patrons or wait staff, including the bartender (or 'tendress—a good-looking brunette in her mid-twenties in the red-plaid shirt and jeans that all the help wore, though she had her top tied into a Daisy Duke's halter).

And I could actually hear some of Janet and Connie's discourse. The nature of the loud music and yelled conversation made it possible to hone in on them, and pick some of it up.

Janet, in her emerald silk blouse and new jeans, was probably the most conservatively dressed woman in the joint—her blowsy gal pal Connie, for instance, was in a low-cut red sweater, an angora number that would've put a big grin on Ed Wood's face, and jeans camel-toe tight.

They were drinking margaritas—on their second round.

And Connie was saying, more or less, "Honey! You should go after it—*really*."

And Janet shook her head and said, "But you're more qualified, Con. Plus, I can think of three people with more tenure than me!"

"*You're* the qualified one, Jan—*you* have the *degree*."

A guy stopped alongside Connie, facing Janet; he was angled enough that it made him a tough read, but I got it: "*My* wife won't have to work."

Rick.

Hadn't recognized him at first—there were dozens of Ricks in Sneaky Pete's. But this was a specific Rick, Rick the prick, the abusive boyfriend who had dropped by the library this afternoon, in his ongoing campaign to make this young woman's life miserable.

Slender, taller than I remembered, he wore a brown leather jacket and black jeans, a glimpse of darker brown shirt beneath. A good-looking guy, as vapid sons of bitches go.

Connie said something I didn't catch, but Rick said, "Fuck you very much" to her, and shoved in beside Janet.

He was turning toward her, so I only got part of his face, but figuring out what he was saying wasn't tough—he wasn't exactly Noel Coward.

"Very funny," he said to her.

She didn't look at him, concentrating on her margarita, or pretending to. "What is?"

"Keeping me waiting."

"Is that what I did?"

"I waited my ass off at the Brew for you, for half a fuckin' hour."

Now she looked at him. Her expression was commendably withering. "We weren't meeting. We didn't have anything set up."

He shook his head, peeved. "So you make me go *lookin'* for you? Lotta bars in this town. That any way to act?"

Connie, staring daggers at their uninvited guest, said, "Do you *mind*? We were *talking*."

He leaned toward the big-hair blonde. "Probably *you* were talking....You mind giving us some privacy?"

"Let me see, let me give that a little thought—how about, I don't frickin' *think* so."

Rick's expression turned menacing. "*I* think so."

Connie looked at Janet.

Janet, reluctantly, nodded to her friend.

Disgusted with both of them, Connie got up and left. She hadn't gone two steps when a guy asked her to dance, and they went out onto the floor and bumped loins to Kenny Chesney.

Rick came around to the other side of the booth, to sit across and make eye contact with Janet, who wasn't cooperating.

Leaning halfway over, he said, "I wasn't kidding, you know. About marriage."

Janet's eyes widened and she began to shake her

head. "The last thing I want to do is marry you, Rick."

"That's not what you said, before."

"That was weeks, maybe months ago. That was when…when you were still being…nice."

"I'm always nice to you!"

She just looked at him.

He shrugged. "Well…I'll be nice in the future. How's that sound?"

"Insincere." Now she leaned forward, and worked hard at softening her expression. "Rick—we're over. You must know that. Can't you see? Let's just walk away friends."

Suddenly he was out of the booth and reaching for her, dragging her out of her seat. He said something I didn't quite catch, but along the lines of: "We're gonna talk this out, *now*."

Then he took her roughly by the arm and hauled her through the bar, toward the door. She was protesting, and I didn't have to read her lips to catch what she said—hell, everybody in the place caught what she said: *"Rick! Please! No…no…."*

Half the eyes in Sneaky Pete's were on the unhappy couple; the other half were making a point of not looking, ignoring what I gathered was a familiar scene around town.

The good-looking brunette bartender was bringing me my third beer. She looked toward the door, and said, "Pity. Hope he doesn't hurt that poor kid, again."

I said, "Isn't anybody going to do anything about it?"

She raised an eyebrow. "You see anybody doing anything about it?"

I threw a five-spot on the counter and said, "Drink that last one yourself."

"Anything you say, Daddy…"

When I was exiting onto the parking lot, half a dozen tobacco addicts were coming back in hurriedly, pitching their smokes sparking into the night. They apparently had no desire to be witnesses to what Rick might do to Janet.

Those two were the only ones in the lot, besides myself, and Rick had her cornered against a big blue Navigator, his hand against the metal, her face turned away from his, eyes shut tight.

"Two people," he shouted at her, "who love each other oughta be able to talk to each other! God! Fuck!"

He used his keys to click open the vehicle's door and shoved Janet in the front seat, rider's side. He was about to shut her in when I put a hand on his shoulder.

Rick whirled, and took a few seconds to size me up—I'm not small, but to him I must have looked no threat, just some ancient asshole sticking his nose in.

He brushed my hand off his shoulder. "Go away. Not your business, dude."

I punched him in the throat.

Rick went down on his knees, clutching his neck, trying to breathe, not having much success, gurgling, his face scarlet, his eyes popping.

From the nearby rider's seat of the SUV, door still open, Janet Wright was taking this in with huge eyes…though not as huge as Rick's.

"Excuse me," I told her, and I took Rick by the collar of his leather jacket and dragged him like the sack of garbage he was across the asphalt. Hauled him through some brush and into the surrounding trees. Deposited him in a small clearing.

Finally able to breathe again, Rick had not, however, found his way up off the ground.

Hurt in more ways than one, he managed to squeak, "You…you coulda *killed* me!"

"No," I said. "Next time I'll kill you."

"What the fuck…fuck business is it…of—"

I bitch-slapped the prick.

The sound surprised me—it was as loud in the night as a gunshot, and the woman in the SUV probably heard it, too. I hoped to hell she wasn't like some abused women, her next move running off and getting her poor abuser some help.

Rick was down on his knees, as if praying. If he really was praying, he was keeping it inside his head, because the "dude" wasn't saying anything—just whimpering.

I knelt before him and I locked my eyes onto his face, though his eyes tried to escape.

"Do you believe I'll kill you?" I asked him.

"Yeah…yeah…sure."

But I wasn't convinced he was convinced.

I took the nine millimeter from my jacket pocket.

He drew in a breath, eyes and nostrils flared.

"Open wide," I said.

"Fuck you!" he said.

The epithet gave me the opening I needed, and I inserted the nine's snout.

I asked him again: "Do you believe I'll kill you?"

Rick, all but deep-throating the barrel, nodded, his eyes white all around, something like "yes, yes" emerging from his throat.

"That's too bad," I said. "Because I really didn't want you to."

And I ripped the gun out of Rick's mouth.

Rick's hand clutched his face and blood streamed through his fingers in little red ribbons. As I'd intended, the weapon's gunsight had carved a notch in the roof of his mouth and maybe chipped a tooth.

He was crying now.

"Anything you'd care to say to me?" I asked.

He lowered his hand; his mouth was a bloody mess, his teeth smeared red; one was, in fact, broken.

Good.

When he spoke, it was through bubbling blood.

"I won't go near her," he said. "Won't ever go near her again."

I shrugged. "Don't decide all at once. Sleep on it."

I whacked him with the nine millimeter and he went to sleep even before he collapsed in a pile in the brush.

The nine's snout had a little blood on it, which I wiped off on the kid's newer-than-new jeans, giving them a little character, wondering if Rick would know, when he woke up, how very lucky he'd been.

I put the gun back in my jacket pocket.

When I came out of the brush and trees, the woman I was here to kill was coming toward me. She was moving steadily, though her expression betrayed an uncertainty about whether she should be afraid or not.

I came to a stop.

She did, too, and asked me, "Is…is he all right?"

"No," I said. "He's a sick fuck."

"Well…" She smiled just a little. "I know that, of course. But you didn't…."

"He'll be fine tomorrow. And I don't think he'll bother you again."

"His family….They're important."

I nodded. "Sent him to the best schools, I bet. But he got his most important lesson tonight….I don't care if his father is named Bush—he won't bother you again."

The brown eyes were wide with worry. "Why did you do that? You...you shouldn't have."

I sighed. "I know."

With no urgency, I took her by the arm and walked her toward the bar.

Her sideways look indicated worry had given way to curiosity. "What's your name?"

"Jack," I said. "Jack Ryan."

"Like in the Tom Clancy novels?"

"Yeah, only a little more heroic."

Her eyebrows lifted. "So I see...."

We were in front of Sneaky Pete's now.

"I'm taking off," I said. "You need a ride anywhere?"

"No...thanks. My friend'll take me home."

I frowned and gestured behind me, toward the trees. "Not *that* friend...."

"No! No. My friend Connie."

She was studying me now, and I felt ill at ease, suddenly. Her face told me what she was thinking— how St. George had just saved her from the dragon, but how strange and even frightening her savior was.

Then her eyes tightened and she spoke. "Were you at the library today?"

"Yes," I said. I gave her a little lame one-finger goodbye salute. "....Good night."

I moved hurriedly to my rental vehicle.

And I could feel her eyes on me, getting in the car and behind the wheel, and even with the window up, I could hear Rick's voice: *"Unnggh....oh...Jesus!"*

He had stumbled from the edge of the wooded area, his mouth bloody, looking like he'd fallen down a couple flights of stairs. He sat on the asphalt, on his knees, prayer-like again, shoulders hunkered over, crying.

I could see Janet thinking about it. She even started toward him, then thought better of it, and yelled, "You deserve it, you dick!"

And she went into the bar.

Starting up the car, I smiled, thinking, *Good for you*.

Then I caught my reflection in my rearview mirror and frowned.

I shoved my hand into the steering wheel, furious with myself, muttering, "Fuck you think you're doing...."

Soon I was pulling into the Homewood Motor Court, which had last been remodeled about five years after Bonnie and Clyde stayed there. Inside, sitting on the edge of my bed with the nine millimeter in one hand and a photo in the other.

I was staring at one of the surveillance shots of Janet Wright, a fairly close-up shot in which she looked not bad at all. I thought about a lot of things, including about how Jonah Green's fucking P.I.

reports didn't even mention this Rick character, but I couldn't work up a healthy sense of indignation, since I was the dipshit who had exposed himself to the target. Saved her from harm and worked up a conversation with her.

Nothing good could come from it—and if this thing went to hell, I'd deserve it. That's what you get for being nice.

I put the photo on the nightstand, image side down. The nine millimeter I shoved under the pillow next to me on the double bed—easier to get to than under your own pillow, plus more comfortable.

Naked, I got between the sheets, shut off the light, but I'd be a fucking liar if I said I went to sleep right away. For a long goddamn time I thought about this young woman, and about what a sweetheart she seemed to be, but that she was dead already, just didn't know it yet, and I shouldn't go all soft in the center or anything, just because she had nice knockers and frilly pink panties.

A long goddamn time.

Five minutes, anyway.

Eight

Janet Wright's apartment—judging by the living room, which was all I could see from my vantage point—indicated an interesting woman lived there: funky '30s deco antiques, a big bookcase of hardcovers, a few striking modern art prints on light green plaster walls. This was a second-floor apartment over a beauty shop, in downtown Homewood, in the last business block before residential kicked in.

She slept in till nine-thirty, and by ten was sitting in a blue terrycloth robe on a big comfy-looking chair with her feet in bunny slippers up on a matching footrest (matching the chair, not the bunny slippers), drinking a cup of what I presumed to be coffee, taking her time, watching television absently.

Finally she got up and went into the next room and quickly came back in a state-college sweatshirt and jeans and went out to run a few errands and have breakfast.

I shadowed her.

Nothing happened.

She returned.

So did I.

The rest of the morning into the early afternoon, hair pinned up, she vacuumed and dusted the living room. At times she disappeared, presumably to have lunch and do laundry somewhere, probably her kitchen area—the apartment seemed to be laid out box-car style, how many rooms I couldn't be sure. The double windows gave me a generous view, but only of the living room.

Judging by my similar apartment, directly across the way, hers would have three big rooms, one after the other, back to the alley. Like hers, my apartment indicated someone interesting lived there—the complicated kind of guy whose decor runs to a metal folding chair with a cushioned seat, a crate near the double window serving as a table (my nine millimeter resting there, and sometimes my binoculars) and a cooler on the bare floor, where already several Coke cans, a wadded-up napkin and a sandwich wrapper lurked.

Unlike Janet's building, this one hadn't been renovated yet, or anyway the upper floors hadn't—the lower floor had been half-heartedly redone but a computer store filling the space was out of business. Homewood had one of those funky downtowns getting gradually rehabilitated, and this empty apartment was, as I said, "similar" to hers…in its positioning and layout.

But there were differences. Her apartment, for

example, was not a hellhole unfit for the foodstamp crowd who'd not long ago been consigned here.

My surveillance roost stank of old food and new ratshit, but it was free, and it was safe—some company of Jonah Green's owned the building and had it earmarked for eventual Yuppification. I'd been provided a key to the back door and an assurance that no nightwatchmen would be checking.

The building across the way mirrored this one, had probably been designed by the same architect and built by the same outfit somewhere after the turn of the century—19th century, that is. Fuck, I was old, having to keep track of goddamn centuries....

Anyway, my target had double windows, too, and she kept the shades up and the sheer, decorative white window dressing blocked almost nothing. She didn't worry about privacy, because you couldn't see in from the street, and the apartment across the way was dead.

But, unlike my swimming-pool surveillance yesterday afternoon, this was no peep show. After the morning of vacuuming, she spent the afternoon sorting and folding laundry, again with the TV on, though I extrapolated that, as my view didn't show it. She also read and listened to music, a CD player nestled in among the hardcovers in the big bookcase. Her comfy chair was near the two windows with a phone stand between.

She had a couple calls, one from Connie setting up another evening out, which interrupted the vacuuming, and another while she was reading.

In both instances, through my binoculars, I saw her checking caller I.D. before picking up—possibly avoiding Rick, although I found it extremely unlikely he'd ever call her again.

Still, she answered the afternoon call warily, then brightened. "Well, Sis!…Sure.…No problem.…Well, that's great!.…Cool!…Play it by ear."

Well, that was scintillating.

A dull call in a dull day, but somehow the mundaneness of her existence was getting to me. You shadow some Outfit cocksucker while he's bouncing between guys he's extorting money from and strip clubs where he's getting free blow jobs, you don't exactly brush a tear away when you remove him from the world. You take out some asshole exec who is embezzling from his bosses to maintain his coke habit, you're over it before you reload. You rid the world of a criminal lawyer who is more crim than law, you feel pretty damn good about your line of work.

But what was a nice girl like her doing in a bad place like this?

I had a Coke habit, too, and half a dozen empty cans were littering my feet by nightfall. This old empty apartment did have a working toilet, which was a nice perk, but I'd overdone the caffeine.

When Janet emerged from a street-level door below, between storefronts, I felt damn near jumpy.

She had disappeared from the living room about an hour and a half before, and the door to the street wasn't within my range of vision, so her change of appearance was a surprise. Nice one.

She looked lovely, the dark blonde hair nicely bouncy, brushing the shoulders of her suede jacket which was a darker brown than her slacks but the same color as her high heels. Barely had she stepped onto the sidewalk than a sporty little red Mazda drew up with gal-pal Connie at the wheel.

Janet got in, they took off, and so did I.

I wasn't thrilled when they went back to Sneaky Pete's—one thing a guy in my trade doesn't like to become is a regular at a joint in a town where he's working. The brunette bartendress welcomed me back like old home week, even asked my name now that I was hanging out so often, and I told her Jack. She asked me a few questions as the evening wore on, and I told her jack.

Janet and Connie had chosen another booth, but the bar was a long one and the mirror behind it, too, so I had no problem setting up reflective watch. I nursed a beer, and did my best not to go over to the jukebox and shoot it—surely there was a limit to how much Toby Keith a reasonable person can endure.

Again Janet wore a silk blouse, a cream-color one,

with a strand of June Cleaver pearls. Her buddy Connie was fetchingly slutty (or did I already have my "beer goggles" on?) in a black-leather motorcycle jacket, red rhinestone-studded Marilyn t-shirt, jeans she wouldn't have to remove when she next went to the gynecologist, and colorful cowboy boots.

Janet seemed embarrassed as Connie leaned forward, eyes and teeth gleaming, saying, "Spill! What happened to Rick?"

"I told you last night I didn't want to talk about' it...." Now Janet sat forward. "Why, what have you heard?"

Connie's grin was unkind. "He's telling his friends he fell down the stairs."

"So, he, uh, didn't...go to the police or anything?"

Connie's eyebrows hiked. "Oh, now you *have* to tell me!"

Janet shook her head, then froze in mid-shake, and said, "Excuse me, Con..."

"Why? What...?"

And something unnerving happened.

Janet's eyes caught mine in the mirror.

Quickly I looked away, and said something inane to the brunette bartender, who complied by saying something equally inane.

I heard Connie yelling, good-naturedly, "You are definitely *not* excused! Janet—you come back here and dish, or *else!*"

I felt the finger tap my shoulder.

I winced, then swung easily around on the bar stool and glanced at her as casually as I could.

"Oh hi," I said.

"Oh hi?" Her smile went up a little more on one side than the other, creating a nice dimpled effect. "I guess I owe you a drink."

"You don't. Really."

"I do. Really."

The stool next to me was vacant; it would be. She took it. We looked at each other in the mirror again, this time on purpose.

She said, "Why do I think you're checking up on me?"

"Why do you?"

For several long seconds she studied me in the mirror, then she said to my reflection, "Well…I imagined I saw you in a booth at Denny's this morning."

"Some imagination you have."

Her eyes were smiling, too. "*Wasn't* it you?"

"That was me. But I wasn't looking for you."

She raised one eyebrow. "You were just there for that delicious Grand Slam breakfast, right?…And now you're here, Guardian Angel, seeing if Rick's had the good sense to…"

"Take a hint?"

Her smile went up on both sides, this time, and

ushered in some laughter. Shaking her head, she said, "I really do owe you one....Have a drink with us."

I didn't want to join her and Connie, and give the other librarian a closer look at me. But I was cornered. Turning Janet down would have been suspicious. Or so I told myself.

Whatever the case, I was soon sitting on Janet's side of the booth as she and bubbly Connie chitchatted, both of them nicely at ease around me, Janet revealing a new self-confidence.

Connie licked some beer foam from her upper lip and, just the tiniest bit drunk, said, "That little prick Rick? He's been a bully since grade school. But he always gets away with it, 'cause his family has money."

"Fuck him," I said. "His family hasn't given me any money."

They both laughed at my naughty talk.

Making reluctant eye contact with Connie, I joined in on the chitchat. "You're from here?"

"Born and raised, and too dumb and untalented to get out." She smirked at Janet, good-naturedly. "What's *your* excuse?"

Janet shrugged and said, "Destiny. Which is to say, answering an ad."

Connie, suddenly quite serious, locked eyes with me. "This little girl's gonna be head librarian one of these days. Just you wait and see."

"Really," I said, and narrowed my eyes and nodded.

Amused, Janet said, "Don't pretend to be impressed—doesn't suit you....And, so, Jack—what is it *you* do?"

"I'm in sales and service," I said.

Janet, apparently the designated driver, was drinking a Diet Coke. "What kind of sales and service?"

"Veterinary medicine."

"That sounds...interesting."

I smiled a little. "No it doesn't."

Connie, frowning, asked, "Do you sell vets that stuff they use to put animals to sleep?"

"Afraid so," I said.

Connie made a face. "Dirty job but...."

"I'm sure," Janet says, "he sells plenty of things that make the animals feel better."

"I try," I said.

Janet and Connie exchanged looks. Connie's smile at her friend told me I'd passed the test—for at least one night. Saturday at Sneaky Pete's, the options were limited.

Janet gave Connie a glance that I didn't at first understand, until Connie straightened herself, her breasts distorting Marilyn Monroe's image but not in a bad way, and said, "You know...I see a guy over there who's just cute enough to interest me, and drunk enough to think likewise...."

She got up and out of the booth less graceful than a ballet dancer, but more fun to watch.

Janet gave me a sideways look. "Now you'll think that's how I spend my weekends."

"What is?"

"You know. Picking guys up."

I offered half a smile. "Have I been?"

Her hands were draped around the Coke glass like it was the Silver Chalice. "It's just…I never had anybody do anything so…*sweet* for me, before."

"Sweet like pound the piss out of your boyfriend?"

I expected a laugh, but what I got was: "Exactly…. I'm not really the type to, I don't know…hit the bars on a Saturday night."

"I know."

Her eyebrows tensed with curiosity. "You do?"

"Today was your day off, right?"

Mildly surprised, Janet said, "Right."

I shrugged. "You cleaned all morning, did laundry all afternoon, and then you listened to music or maybe read, a while. You fell asleep and were almost late to go out with your girlfriend."

Astonished, she said, "My God—are you psychic?"

"No." I toasted her with my beer glass. "I'm shadowing you."

That got a smile and a laugh out of her. The truth will do that.

She was shaking her head. "I'm just not good at this. The game. The ritual. The small talk's all so…"

"Small," I said.

Get 2 Books Every Month...
For the Price of ONE!

☐ **YES! Sign me up for the Hard Case Crime Book Club!**

As long as I choose to stay in the club, I will receive TWO Hard Case Crime books each month — that month's latest title plus an earlier title from the Hard Case Crime archives. I'll get to preview each month's titles for 10 days. If I decide to keep them, I will pay only $6.99* each month — a savings of 50%! There is no minimum number of books I must buy and I may cancel my membership at any time.

Name: _____

Address: _____

City / State / ZIP: _____

Telephone: _____

E-Mail: _____

☐ **I want to pay by credit card:** ☐ VISA ☐ MasterCard ☐ Discover

Card #: _____ Exp. date: _____

Signature: _____

Mail this card to:
HARD CASE CRIME BOOK CLUB
20 Academy Street, Norwalk, CT 06850-4032

Or fax it to 610-995-9274.
You can also sign up online at www.dorchesterpub.com.

* Plus $2.00 for shipping. Offer open to residents of the U.S. and Canada only. Canadian residents please call 1-800-481-9191 for pricing information.

If you are under 18, a parent or guardian must sign. Terms, prices, and conditions subject to change. Subscription subject to acceptance. Dorchester Publishing reserves the right to reject any order or cancel any subscription.

"I guess....I've always been kind of shy, frankly. A loner."

"Me, I'm a people person."

Another smile. "Oh, yeah, I can see that," she said.

"You often...gravitate toward people like Rick?"

Her smile was gone and a smirk took its place. "Connie says it's low self-esteem. I say it's bait and switch...guys on their best behavior when they meet you, but who aren't really, you know..."

"What they seem?"

Suddenly she sat up, something obviously occurring to her. She checked her watch.

"Shit," she said.

"Was it something I said?"

"No! No, no, there's just....Look, there's something I have to do, something that slipped my mind, I should've done earlier."

"You need a lift somewhere? Your friend seems busy."

Connie was flirting with a guy over by the jukebox, which was having the good if rare sense to play a Patsy Cline song, "Crazy."

Janet was shaking her head, saying, "Well, you see, I'm sort of semi-housesitting...for some friends of mine? Anyway, I need to bring in their mail, and their dog's probably half-starved....Somehow after last night, with Rick, I just...spaced out on it, today."

"I see."

She gave me a look that had some pleading in it. "I don't want to bother Con. Would you mind...driving me out there?"

"Sure," I said, getting out of the booth, and helping her do so, too. "But you'll have to show me the way."

Nine

She was a tad over-dressed, in that silk blouse, for watering the plants, but the plants didn't seem to mind, and I certainly didn't.

I followed her around as dutifully as a dog—she'd already fed the real dog, and put it on a leash and walked it, and I'd kept her company on those chores, too—and we'd already worked through a lot of small talk about the library and her friend Connie and a little bit about Rick, who she actually sort of felt sorry for (I let her get away with that) (for now) and currently she was filling me in on this beautiful house itself, which was as wood and stone inside as out, including a hall fountain that was like water rushing over mountain rocks.

I asked when the place was built, and she said, "In the fifties some time, by my friend's father…my friend, Dave Winters—he owns the office furniture plant, that keeps Homewood going? This is his house now, his and Lisa's….I met Dave at college."

Following her to the next plant, I said, "I thought you weren't a local girl."

"I'm not," she said, taking care not to over-water. She was using a little red watering can from the kitchen. "Dave's on the library board—when my application came in, he recognized the name of course, and helped me get the job. His wife is great, too."

"Lisa," I said.

She frowned at me. "How do you know Lisa?"

"I don't. You mentioned her, before."

"Oh."

And on to the next plant.

"Where are the Winters?"

She flicked me a longing little glance. "Nassau. A little month-long getaway."

"Must be nice."

Sighing, she moved to a corner where a palm-tree-like number waited; from the size of it, this triffid could have walked to the kitchen to get its own goddamn water.

She was saying, "Hard not to envy Lisa and Dave—swimming and sunning and swimming and sunning and eating wonderful food and swimming and sunning some more."

"Wouldn't that suck," I said.

She finished her rounds and I followed her to the kitchen, where she replaced the watering can under the sink. Turning to me with a lilting smile, she asked, "I bet you like to swim. You're a swimmer, aren't you?"

I frowned with my forehead and smiled with my mouth. "What are you, psychic?"

"No." Her smile turned mischievous. "Maybe I've got *you* under surveillance...."

The swimming pool room seemed even larger when you were in there, an echoey cavernous dark-wood space with the lighted swimming pool a blue shimmering centerpiece.

Janet, in a light blue one-piece bathing suit, balanced at the tip of the diving board, bouncing a little, dark-blonde locks flouncing when I came in from the dressing room in a suit two sizes two small for me. Well, it made the package look bigger, anyway, even if it did cut off my circulation. Of course, cutting off the circulation would eventually not do the package any favors, either.

She didn't say anything just grinned and bounced and laughed and bounced and laughed and grinned.

"Glad you're having such a good time," I said.

"Sorry....Dave's not...not a big man."

"Just in business," I said, eyeing the vast chamber. I was standing at the edge of the pool like a guy on a building ledge contemplating suicide. I pointed casually toward her. "That Dave's wife's suit?"

"Yes. Lisa and me, we're about the same size."

"She has a nice figure."

"Lisa thanks you, I'm sure."

With this, she dove in, an admirable, even elegant dive.

Even so, she splashed me some, doing it; but I

didn't mind. The flecks of water were quite warm, really, even inviting.

I dove in.

The pool was as warm as a bath, lulling—actually, I prefer it a little crisper, but this was nice. Very nice.

For a while we swam, doing a few laps together, sometimes underwater or on our backs, and splashed and clowned around, the kind of capering kids get in trouble for from the lifeguard, only there was no lifeguard present. We laughed and teased and talked, enjoying the usual pleasing swimming-chamber hollow effect.

We were treading water, facing each other, when I said, "Nice perk, for semi-housesitting."

"Swimming's the best."

"Oh yeah," I agreed sincerely.

A little out of breath, face droplet-pearled, she could hardly have looked more lovely, even though the long hair was matted down with moisture, the makeup mostly gone from her heart-shaped face, an indicator of just what a striking woman this was.

Paddling there, blinking the big brown eyes, she said, "Nothing quite relaxes you like a nice swim. Really takes you somewhere else."

"Couldn't agree more."

Treading doggedly, maybe a little tired now and having to work at it some, she said, "I mean, I don't envy Dave and Lisa much, but to have this handy, right in your own house? To be able to—de-stress any time you like, and just feel...really *free*..."

"You know," I said, a tiny bit out of breath myself, "you shouldn't swim here by yourself. Dangerous."

She laughed, treading water, more and more an effort. "What? You think I'm gonna dive in and klunk my stupid head?"

I plunge her head under water, my hand gripping the top of her skull and shoving her down, and holding her there; she struggles but can't get anywhere, arms and legs flailing with fading force.

Finally, she is limp, dead weight, and I release her, and let her float to the surface, arms spread, reaching for nothing, tendrils of hair spreading like seaweed.

"Hey!" she said, bobbing there. "Aren't you listening? Where did *you* go?"

"Somewhere else," I admitted. "For a second."

"I was just saying, I can fix you something, if you like. Have you eaten?"

Soon we were in the Winters' kitchen, sitting on stools at the counter in our respective robes (hers blue and fitting nice, mine white and, again, two sizes too small, my shoulders straining the seams), eating microwave dinners and drinking Diet Cokes. Nearby, the penned-up dog, although fully fed not forty-five minutes ago, was whining pitifully, as if it hadn't had a meal since summer.

Janet, gnawing a leg of Swanson chicken, said, "Toss her a scrap, why don't you?"

I speared a bite of Salisbury steak. "What, and spoil the bitch?"

"You're evil."

I didn't feel like contradicting her.

We had cleaned up after ourselves, and were standing at the sink like an old married couple when I asked, "What do you have on under that robe?"

Her smile was pixie-ish. "Wouldn't you like to know?…What do you have under yours?"

I opened mine and showed her. It was a good thing I wasn't wearing David's tiny trunks.

"You can get arrested in some states for that," she said, but her eyes were big and pleased.

I opened the front of her robe and saw the creamy skin and lovely breasts and the wonderful Old School muff.

"That's illegal in most states," I said. "Pubic nakedness."

"That's *public* nakedness. And, anyway, this is private."

I slipped the robe off her shoulders and let it slip down her narrow-waisted, full-hipped frame to puddle on the floor at her bare feet.

"Yeah," I said. "Isn't it?"

In the Winters Family Rec Room, I took the time to get a fire going in the big rough-stone fireplace while Janet waited, naked underneath an Indian blanket. Then I joined her and we necked a while, romantically. When I finally kissed her breasts, the nipples were erect, damn near an inch long and hard, so hard. I kissed her neck, she kissed mine. I put my hand between her legs and the moistness there wanted attention. I buried my head down there and licked and sucked; then her head was in my lap and she licked and sucked. Things were getting serious.

"On top of me," she whispered, her face looking up at me half-lidded, mouth open in terrible, exquisite pain. "On top...."

For all the moistness, she was tight—a little hand might have been gripping me down there—and she shuddered and cried in pain and delight as I entered her and slid myself slowly in and out. I cupped the full firm globes of her ass and nuzzled her breasts as she moved her hips in ways she hadn't learned in the library, the inside of her sucking out the inside of me. The blanket had fallen away, and our flesh was reflecting the licking flames, one body with many limbs and so much skin, blushed orange, and after a while her eyes rolled up in her head so that barely anything but white showed as I plunged in and out of her with the blade of flesh.

We hadn't talked about protection—we were just naked and together and the lust ran away with us and

I'd been in her. And now my seed was in her, too. Some detached voice in my head said, *She's already dead, she doesn't need protection....*

Then we were on top of the blanket. The fire had dwindled to a nice comfort level, and we were wrapped up in a post-coital embrace, sleepy, at ease with each other, so much so that we could just laugh as we picked pubic hairs off our respective tongues. My efforts to cough one up off the back of my throat almost made her hysterical.

After while she had quieted down enough to ask, "Were you a soldier?"

"How did you know that? Surveillance?"

Her smile was sweet for a girl who'd just given me a royal fucking. She shook her head. "I just feel it, *know* it, somehow....My grandfather was in Korea. You remind me of him."

"Well, that's made my day."

She laughed and her face crinkled apologetically. "No, no, no, I didn't mean...*that*."

She studied me; touched my face with a finger. Examining me. Like I was an old tree, cut in half, whose rings you could count.

Finally, over the sound of a crackling fireplace, she asked, "Vietnam? Are you that old? You couldn't be that old."

"But I am."

"How is that possible?"

I shrugged. "I was a baby when I went in."

She nodded wisely. "But not when you came out."

"…I was stupid."

Her brow tensed. " 'Stupid,' how?"

I shook my head. "*Real* stupid. Married a girl on leave, in San Diego? When I got home, she was fucking this guy."

"Oh dear," she said, as if reacting to my harsh language, which in part maybe she was. Her fingertips came to her lips, a dainty gesture for a girl who'd had my cock in her mouth not long ago. "I'm so sorry.…What did you do?"

I shrugged again. "I went over to talk to him. Just reason with him. He was working under his car."

Her brow tightened further. "What did you do?"

"Kicked the jack out."

She didn't draw away or anything. Didn't even blink. Just asked, "…You got in trouble?"

One more shrug. "I didn't do much time. But I was a kid, and didn't understand."

Nodding, Janet said, "You mean, how your wife could do that to you?"

"I mean, why killing people I didn't know, in some other country, people who didn't deserve it particularly, was cool. But kill one jackass back home who earned it, and I get shit."

Her look of compassion, of sympathy, was so sincere, I could barely stand it.

She said, "I'm so sorry....You don't have to talk about it."

Surprised, I said, "I almost never do."

I had opened up to her as I had my Vietnam pal Gary, who was the only other human about whom that could be said; even my late wife, the second one—the nice, stupid one—I'd never shared it with. *Why the fuck had I tonight?* Couldn't be the little head controlling me, because it was all tuckered out down there.

Or anyway I thought it was.

Because all of a sudden Janet was crawling up on top of me, kissing me on the chest and the neck and then on the face, and the view of her, all that pale flesh, those breasts hanging down so full and beautifully shaped and gently swaying with those long tips sticking out at me accusingly, well, it woke the little head up, all right.

This time, however, having climbed on top, she stayed there. She was ready to take a little control.

And I was ready for somebody to take it.

Ten

Having been up and dressed a while, I was in the kitchen, at the stove scrambling eggs (bacon already made), when she drifted in in the blue terrycloth robe, hair looking nicely tousled.

Sleepily sexy, she paused to lean in the doorway and sniff the cooking smells approvingly.

"Wow," she said. "You're a surprise."

"Coffee's ready," I said.

She made her way over to the counter where the Cuisinart coffee-maker dripped and helped herself to a cup.

The dog was penned up, and—despite the cooking smells—sleeping in its bed.

"What did you do?" she asked, nodding toward the dog, the mug of coffee in both hands, blowing at it a little. "Drug the mutt?"

"No. Just fed it. All it wanted."

She laughed and risked a sip.

"Been walked, too," I said. "But I draw the line at that pooper-scooper crap."

"Even so," she said, "you definitely pass the audition." She settled on a stool at the counter as I served her up eggs and bacon and toasted, buttered English muffins.

"Eggs are *good*," she said.

"Thanks," I said, serving myself, then joining her. "Everybody has to learn *something* from their mother."

We ate a while, then between bites she asked, "How long you been awake?"

I shrugged. "Two, three hours."

She blinked at me; her eyes were puffy—but on her, it looked good. "It's only seven-something now."

"Went for groceries. Had a swim."

She gave me a sideways look. "You really like to swim....Helps you think?"

"Helps me not to think."

We ate in silence for a while, and somehow it became a little awkward or maybe pregnant. Which served me right, not using a rubber last night....

Finally, she pushed her almost-cleaned plate away, and got up and got herself some more coffee and refilled my cup, saying, "I, uh...really don't do this kind of thing."

"Wait on men?"

She laughed a little. "No...you know." She sat next to me again, sipped the coffee, raised an eyebrow. "I mean, I hardly know you. I just don't usually..."

"Kiss on the first date?"

She smiled over the coffee cup's lip. "Kiss on the first date."

I pushed my plate away. Sipped coffee. Said, "I live alone, too."

Her brow tensed. "Sorry. I...I don't follow you."

"Sometimes you just...need something."

She thought about that, and nodded. It was a sort of admission.

"There really haven't been a lot of 'Ricks,' " she said. "Some. But mostly, the last eight, ten years... I've kept to myself."

"Safer that way," I said.

"You, too?"

"...It's the easiest way to get hurt."

"Also the most painful," she said quickly. "When I was younger, I went with older guys...?"

I hiked an eyebrow. "And things have changed?"

"Well, you're the first...'older guy'...in some time. A shrink once told me I have some kind of 'daddy' complex."

I shifted in my seat.

I shrugged. "Every little girl wants to fuck her daddy. And lots of daddies want to fuck their little girls. It only counts against you when you go through with it."

She thought about that, then said, "You...scare me a little."

I gave her half a smile. "Just a little?"

She studied me and something devilish got into her eyes. "You might not be so scary, naked."

"You've seen me naked."

She shook her head. "Oh no, I haven't...."

Soon we were seated on the edge of the pool in our borrowed swimsuits, the place muggy as hell, a virtual steamroom, and she was about to apply a straight razor to my well-lathered beard.

"Be gentle," I said.

"Don't worry," she said, and kept her word, starting to shave me gently, tenderly, sliding, gliding the blade, taking whiskers, leaving smooth flesh. Occasionally she would dip the razor in the pool, getting rid of whiskery lather.

It took a while, my beard not terribly long but full, and it felt good, being the object of such care and attention; but when the blade pressed against my throat, I caught her wrist, stopping her.

For all the heat, we froze, my eyes locked with hers, and I wasn't smiling as I stared at her—she seemed quietly amused, if a bit taken aback by the clutch of my hand.

"What's wrong, Jack?" She seemed wholly serious, but for a pixie gleam in the eyes. "Don't you trust me?"

Now I studied her, tried to look inside—*did she know why I was here?*—and her amusement faded to concern.

I said, "Little tender there. Let me."

"Sure."

She gave me the razor.

As I finished the shave, she sat next to me, slightly shaken, holding her arms to herself as if feeling a sudden chill.

We did not make love again. Janet had to work today—it was Sunday, but the Homewood Library was open from eleven till four—and she needed to go to her apartment to shower and change. I dropped her in front of the beauty shop she lived over, and—before she got out—she said, "I'll never forget last night, Jack."

"Good," I said, and managed to smile.

Her eyes stayed on me a beat too long before she got out of the car. I thought I detected something hurt in the expression, but wasn't sure.

Maybe I decided to take Sunday off. Maybe that was it. But that afternoon, as Janet no doubt did routine work at the library and maybe did her story-hour shtick with another third-grade audience, I wasn't around to see it.

I was in my motel room, feeling bare with my freshly shaved face, on my back on the bed, elbows winged out, staring at the ceiling, lights off, sun filtering in a little through closed drapes. Janet's picture on the nightstand, face down. Nine millimeter on the nightstand.

By late afternoon, with the library closing so early,

she'd be back at her apartment. And somehow I hauled my dead ass off that bed and made it to my surveillance roost across the way from her.

She beat me home. There she was, already, in a bathrobe again (not the blue borrowed one, but a similar green one of her own), sitting in that comfy chair, bunny-slippered tootsies on the footrest, reading a book (*Memoirs of a Geisha*), nibbling a sandwich, sipping at a Diet Coke.

But I was having trouble watching her.

Mostly I just sat there, staring at the blank wall in the rattrap vacant apartment, not even dipping into the cooler for my own sandwich and Coke, not fucking hungry at all. The nine millimeter and the binoculars were on the crate, looking like decorative items as opposed to anything practical a person might actually use.

I did at dusk, at a good distance, follow her Geo to Sneaky Pete's, which was open Sunday nights, where she and Connie met in the parking lot. I drove past, then pulled a U-turn and headed back.

Inside, the place wasn't very busy, the meat-market aspect given over to a modest family night, where pizza was served from a small kitchen that usually only offered up burgers and fries. The same country-pop was playing, but overlaid with the squeal of kiddies, and it occurred to me it might do the Sneaky Pete singles crowd of Friday and Saturday night some good, stopping by here Sunday, just to see what kind of trouble they might be getting themselves into.

Janet and Connie had a booth, both young women dressed not to the nines now, just sweatshirts and jeans; this was about dinner and dishing, Connie pumping Janet for what had happened between her and "that big scary handsome guy."

That was the only thing I picked up, from my position at the bar. I couldn't risk sitting any closer, and I was conspicuous as hell in this family crowd. Even the bartender, not my familiar brunette but a potbellied guy with a mustache, was giving me a hinky look. So unless I wanted to be spotted and invited over to sit with the girls, I had better split.

I split.

Back at the motel, the room was nicely dark, just a little neon sign blush finding its way through the curtains. I deposited the nine on the nightstand and flopped onto the bed, fully clothed, curled up on my side and tried to go to sleep.

But it soon became clear sleep wouldn't come, and before long I found myself seated on the edge of the bed, slumped, hands loosely interlaced.

What were my fucking options?

Piss and poor, with maybe a couple stops in between. This was what I got, allowing myself to be talked out of retirement for "one last job." Fuck!

There are reasons why you quit the killing business, and going soft is one of them, because then it's you getting killed, which is no way to run a business.

They were my Achilles' heel, women. I had no goddamn sense where they were concerned. And it wasn't the fucking, the fucking was great, but a woman—not just any woman, but a woman like, say, Janet—could touch something inside of me that I liked to think had died a long time ago. Something human that could only put a dipshit like me in a jam.

I sat there, brooding, mentally listing the mistakes I'd made, but the list was so long, I got bored—being seen by the target was one thing, eating her pussy was another. That kind of up-close-and-personal contact can lead a guy to making bad calls.

So I could walk away. You can always walk away.

And someone else would kill her, and Jonah Green would, understandably, be miffed with me, and likely send people to kill me, loose end that I would become, people like me but not old and gone-soft ones, and then I'd be dead, too…or at least up to my asshole in dead assholes.

That didn't sound like any fun.

I could go after the guy who hired me. I had full confidence that I could make Jonah Green's death happen; but Green was an important guy, connected enough in Outfit circles to find out about my past, and with the wherewithal to find me at Sylvan Lake in short order. I killed him, who could say what the fuck I'd unleash?

And I'd be dead, and Janet Wright would be dead, too.

That left only one alternative: go ahead and do the job I'd been hired for. There was that little matter of a quarter of a million dollars, the kind of money that meant I'd never have to put myself in a situation like this again.

And if I accepted that Janet Wright was really dead already, just didn't know it yet—a premise I had expressed to Jonah Wright at the outset, a concept I knew to be true when any party had been marked for elimination—perhaps the only humane thing to do under the circumstances was kill her myself.

I could figure out some way that would be quick and painless. If I left her to the devices of some amoral monster who killed people for money, Christ knew *what* shit she would be put through....

I had always taken great pride in my lack of sadism, that I had never taken any sick pleasure or joy out of turning life into death. Mine had been a profession, and like a doctor with a patient or a lawyer with a client, I represented a person with a problem, and I just made that problem go away. Nothing fun about it. Nothing mean about it, either.

Such were my thoughts, threading through my

brain and the motel-room darkness, and I don't honestly remember going to Janet's. In my mind, I'm in the motel room one second, sitting on the bed, trying to figure this shit out, and the next second, I'm at the top of the stairs out on the small landing, staring at her apartment door, with the nine millimeter in one hand and working the doorbell with the other.

She didn't answer.

Well, it was the middle of the night; or rather, really, really early Monday morning....

So I rang it again.

And again.

Finally I could hear her moving in there.

I checked the action on the nine.

The sound of the night latch unlatching prompted me to slip the nine back in my jacket pocket, and then her face, pale and severe without makeup, was visible in the cracked-open door.

She frowned just a little. "...Jack?"

"I have to see you."

She frowned more than just a little. "You know, even *Rick* used to call the day after. Even *Rick* never showed up at three in the morning, demanding—"

"Please?"

She sighed.

She let me in.

Wrapped up in the green robe, which was feminine but not particularly sexy, Janet seemed embarrassed by my intrusion, self-consciously straightening her hair.

"Sit down," she said, leading me into a living room that I'd never been in before, though was entirely familiar with. "Give me a minute...freshen up." She turned toward me, not mad at all, now. "You want coffee or something? Jesus, what time *is* it?"

I took her into my arms, firmly but not roughly, and asked, "What time does it have to be?"

And I kissed her.

The kiss was a little over the top, zero-to-sixty kind of thing, and it surprised her; but she got into it, soon enough.

I lowered her to the floor, and I drew open the robe and she was almost afraid, looking up at me, and her throat was red, her face white, her breasts full and staring at me.

Then my pants were around my ankles and I was fucking her. Her knees were up and she was saying, "Oh, oh, oh," really liking it; but halfway through I slowed it down and kissed her neck and breasts and ears and shoulders and face, and she was crying, and maybe I was crying, what the fuck are you going to do about it?

The finish was slow and gentle and, again, I don't remember going there, but we were in bed, Janet sleeping contentedly next to me, snuggling to me. Killing her in her sleep would have been so easy. Not the accident Green had requested, but painless and she would never know a thing.

But I wasn't about to kill her.

She was coming alive, this woman, she'd been sleepwalking through a coma of a life, and now she was alive, and killing her would have been a god-damn crime. I had a new agenda I was working on, but a wonderful tiredness had me suddenly, and then I was asleep, too.

The next thing I felt was a hand gently caressing my neck, and then I heard Janet, saying, "Hey, Samson—wake up a second."

My eyes somehow opened, and she was sitting on the edge of the bed, in a white blouse and dark skirt, smelling great, but ready for work, not for me.

I sat bolt upright, startling her a little, though she laughed.

"Hey! Hey, relax....I'm leaving for the library. Thought I'd better see if you have anywhere to be."

I tasted my mouth; it wasn't worth the effort. "No. No appointments....Can I just crash here?"

"Sure." She stood, smoothed herself, looking pro-fessional and adult, whereas I felt like a kid sleeping in instead of going to school. "I'll leave the extra key on the kitchen table, if you wanna go in or out."

"When'll you be home?"

"I get off at five, today. Don't *you* fix supper—I will!"

"Listen—Janet...."

She was poised at the door to the kitchen, and turned to me, eyebrows arched. "Yes?"

"Tonight....We have to talk."

Her mouth twitched with amusement. "Isn't that usually the *woman's* line?...Or maybe you just want to explain why a guy selling veterinary medicine carries a gun."

That sucker-punched me, and I glanced over at the chair where my corduroy jacket was draped and saw the nine mil's butt sticking up out of the pocket.

When I turned back to Janet, she'd gone.

I ran after her, bare-ass, but she was already out the kitchen door and on her way across the alley to the lot were she parked her Geo.

Over the next hour or so, I showered and made myself a little breakfast, and tried to get my thoughts together. How much did she know about me? When had she noticed the nine millimeter—just now? She sure didn't seem worked up about it....

All the days of surveillance, and being on top of her in more ways than one, I still had no idea why anyone on the planet, much less a mogul like Jonah fucking Green, would want this sexy little librarian wasted. The only thing she was guilty of was shitty taste in men.

By late morning, I was pacing in her living room, the nine stuffed in my waistband. I'd come to a decision—I would tell Janet some kind of story that stopped well short of the truth, but would be enough to motivate her; and I would grab her and haul her ass out of here, to safety somewhere.

And I would deal with Jonah Green, and everything that meant. Killing the guy who hired you is a non-starter in my business, but then I was ready to retire again, anyway, so what the fuck.

But why wait?

The sooner I got Janet out of Homewood, the better. I would go yank her out of that library, run her back here to pick up a few things, and we'd be on the road. That was the plan. That was the new plan....

And I was just about to go out the door and head down to the street, where my rental was parked, when somebody on the other side of that door began to work a key in it.

I took a step back, and the door swung rudely open, and standing framed there, key in hand, was a young woman who was not Janet, but an attractive enough example of the female sex, even though her ragged jeans and a jean jacket and a black hip-hop t-shirt didn't do much for me.

I knew this woman, this girl. And so do you—she was, after all, the kidnap victim who started it all.

Jonah Green's daughter—Julie.

Eleven

I grabbed the little bitch by the arm extending the key and yanked her into the living room and hurled her across the room. Her jean jacket came off in my hand, and I discarded it like a used tissue as she did a half spin and landed rudely on the couch, opposite, breasts bobbling under the black t-shirt. A little suitcase was out in the hall, and I grabbed it and tossed it inside the apartment, and slammed the door and turned to glare at her.

But she didn't scare easy, scrambling back off the cushions to get right in my face, holding the keys in her upraised fist like a blade. Eyes and nostrils flaring, white little feral teeth bared, she all but screamed: "What the fuck are *you* doing here?"

The petite dark-haired beauty had a little ring in her nose now; she was packing enough piercings to set off an airport metal detector.

As would my nine millimeter automatic, the snout of which I stuck under her defiant chin as I slapped the keys rattlingly from her fist.

"You first," I said.

That took some of the fearlessness out of her. Her eyelids were quivering and she swallowed, or tried to. "Get…get that fucking thing out of my throat, you prick."

I did, shoving her back onto the couch with my free hand. Looming over her, keeping the nine trained on her, I paced a little area near where she sat, her arms folded tight as she looked up at me, face blank but for a crinkly chin.

"Explain yourself," I said.

"Fuck you!…I'm visiting my sister."

I frowned down at her. "Where?"

"Here!" Her eyes widened and tightened. "Where the hell else? She *lives* here!"

My eyes narrowed and tightened. "In this apartment…?"

"No, in a dumpster out back." She unfolded her arms, leaning forward on the heels of her hands. "What the hell are you *doing* here, Quarry?"

I was still pointing the gun at her, but suddenly I felt way off my game. "What's your sister's name?"

"You're in her apartment and you don't know? Janet Fucking Wright!"

I squinted at her, hoping that would help; it didn't. I could see neither a resemblance in her face, nor any sense in this situation.

"Your name is *Green*," I said.

"Aren't you the observant son of a bitch?" She sighed impatiently. "Jan doesn't use Daddy's name— she fucking hates Daddy, which is the one thing we have in common....Wright's our mom's maiden name. *Late* mom..."

Suddenly her face whitened, as if she'd finally noticed an asshole was pointing a gun at her.

"Oh shit," she said, pointing a gun-like finger back at me, for nobody's benefit in particular. "Oh hell. Oh *no*...."

"What?"

She was shaking her head, almost frantically. "You're not 'him,' are you? You couldn't be *him*...." She rolled her eyes and laughed harshly. "Oh fuck *me*....Jack? You're *Jack*? Jack Ryan...?"

I lowered the nine a hair. "She told you about me?"

Still shaking her head, she said, "Oh Christ— *you're* her white knight? Kill me. Kill me now."

"It's an option," I said.

Not knowing how much trouble she was potentially in, Julie sneered up at me. "I answered your question, now you owe *me* a fucking answer—what the hell are you doing here, anyway?"

She had a point.

I put the gun in my waistband. I could see no reason not to level with her. More or less.

I sat next to her and said, "Your father hired me."

She gave me a frowning sideways look, not so much disapproving as curious. "What'd he hire you for? Oh fuck...tell me it wasn't to rough up that abusive boyfriend of hers! That prick Rick?"

I shook my head. "That was my bright idea."

She grunted a non-laugh. "Not that Daddy would do anything that thoughtful." Confusion colored her features. "Then *why*—"

"Your father hired me to watch your sister. He didn't say why."

Her eyes narrowed. "Just watch her—like a P.I. or something?"

"Or something."

A little half-hearted laugh made the cupcake breasts bounce; you could see the nipple rings outlined against the black t-shirt. "Well, I can't say it surprises me."

"Why not?"

"Don't you know?" She leaned toward me conspiratorially. "Sis is about to come into a good share of the family fortune."

I said nothing.

My expression must have been talkative, though, because a faintly amused Julie Green said, "Huh… You look *shocked*, Quarry…I didn't know you were the fuck shockable."

Normally I wasn't.

"I liked you better with the beard, by the way," she said. She got up and collected her jeans jacket and laid it over a chair, and picked up her little suitcase and put it next to the same chair.

"It was your sister's idea," I said. "She shaved me."

She glanced at me, smirky but not unfriendly. "I bet she did....You okay?"

"Peachy."

Over the years, in my business, I'd run into lots of things, many of them disgusting or creepy or downright evil. A father hiring a hitman to take out his own daughter had just rocketed to the top of my personal chart.

With a bullet.

Twelve

Julie Green and I sat in her sister's tiny kitchen where the girl had a turkey sandwich and chips and a Diet Coke; I just had a Diet Coke, my appetite dulled somehow. She filled me in, chapter and verse, on the Green family fortune and how it impacted Daddy and his daughters.

Seemed Green's media empire had started when he married money—that money belonging to the late mother of Janet and Julie.

"It's a trust fund deal," Julie was saying, nibbling at the white bread and white turkey meat. She could wear hip-hop clothes all she wanted—this kid was Caucasian. "Jan's gonna be thirty next month, and she'll get a pile."

"What about you?"

She grinned as she chewed. "Oh, I will, too, when I'm her age....I still got a few years of youthful abandon left."

I was squinting again, but this time things were coming into focus. "And if something bad happened to Janet—before the trust fund money came available to her—your father inherits…?"

"Yeah. Sure. Who else?"

One aspect remained fuzzy, however, so I asked, "But why would that matter to a mogul like Jonah Green? He's *loaded*...."

She snorted a laugh, and the nose ring jiggled. "He *was*, before his second wife's settlement...and before he invested in fucking Enron. He's riding on fumes, my clean-shaven friend. Hope you enjoyed your hundred K for rescuing me, 'cause the bastard made me give him an I.O.U. for it!"

I leaned back in the hard kitchen chair. Sipped my Coke and mulled this new information.

Julie sat forward. "Okay, what wheels are turning in that fucked-up skull of yours?...Quarry, are you trying figure out a way to make a buck again? Squeeze Daddy over Janet?"

I flicked her a little frown.

Her eyes went big and her smile was big, too. "Don't *tell* me...don't tell me you really *fell* for my dowdy ol' big sis...? The degenerate hardass and the maiden librarian ....Didn't I see that on *Lifetime*?"

"I'm going to help her," I said.

She didn't seem to be sure whether to be amused by that or not, and just asked, "Help her where *Daddy's* concerned? How the fuck?"

"Will you help me do it?"

She smirked. "Sure. Do *what*?"

"Will...*you*...*help*?"

She shrugged magnanimously. "Sure—why the

fuck not? My sister is the only relative on the planet that I give two shits about, and anything that gives Daddy a bad day is my idea of a good time."

"Swell." I rose. "I'm going to call her at the library."

"Okay." She watched me go to the kitchen's wall phone. "You want privacy?"

"No."

The library was on a short list of numbers posted by the phone (Rick's had a line through it; mine at the motel was added on) and I dialed.

"Homewood Public Library," Janet's voice said pleasantly. "Help Desk, this is Ms. Wright, how may I help you?"

"Like you did last night," I said, "is just fine."

Her voice warmed up. "Hi, Jack."

"Listen," I said lightly. "Your sister dropped by the apartment, and we're getting along famously."

"Oh! Completely forgot about Jules! I should've mentioned her, Jack, sorry…but she didn't say when exactly she was coming. She's kind of a…you know, free spirit."

I glanced over at Julie. She was standing next to the kitchen table, now, slipping out of the t-shirt. She tossed it on the table and stood there grinning at me, fists Superman-style on her hips, the nice little pierced-nippled breasts bare and perky and proud.

My dick twitched.

"Free spirit, huh?" I said to the girl's sister. "I

noticed....How about after work the three of us meet for a drink, grab a bite together?"

"Great! I'll go straight to Sneaky Pete's, unless you're sick of it."

"No, that's fine. See you there."

We exchanged 'byes, I hung up, and the little topless punkette was right there, right on me, wrapping her arms around me, pushing me to the wall, cornering me like she had at Harry and Louis's cabin.

"I'm not on the rag *now*," she said with a wicked smile and a single arched eyebrow. "You finally ready for that reward?"

I put my hands on her hips, held her away from me at arm's length, and took a long, leering look at her and she grinned, pleased with herself.

Then I pushed her away. "Get your shirt on before your nipple rings rust."

She backed off and appraised me, frowning; now I finally could see the resemblance between the sisters—the tips of Julie's breasts were long, too.

"Turning me down again, Quarry?"

"I seem to be."

I wasn't sure if that had been a test or if she was just a little cockhound.

Maybe the former, because after she slipped the black t-shirt on, she winked at me and said, "Okay. Okay. Maybe you really *do* like my big sis."

Thirteen

Monday night at Sneaky Pete's was slow, the singles crowd modest and the laughter and conversation lessened, which only made the country western schlock on the jukebox all the more noticeable. I did my best to control the situation by plowing quarters in and selecting the Patsy Cline, Hank Williams and Willie Nelson numbers, trying to hold the crap at bay.

I had thought Janet chose the bar because it had somehow become "our" place; but I soon realized she'd made the choice to accommodate her sister, who drank more than she ate. Our burgers hadn't even arrived yet, and Julie was already on her second Scotch rocks.

Janet was on my side of the booth, looking fondly at her sister and me and back again, working a little too hard to get a family vibe going.

"So," she asked, "you two already *know* each other? How is that possible?"

Julie shrugged, glugged Scotch, and said, "He got me out of a jam, a while back."

Janet cocked her head, eyes flicking from her sister to me to her sister. "What kind of jam, Jules?"

Julie shrugged again. "Some assholes kidnapped me."

At that Janet laughed. Then, studying the dark-haired, nose-pierced girl, asked, "You're…not kidding, are you?"

Julie shook her head. "No. Some assholes grabbed me to squeeze ransom money out of Daddy. Our, uh, mutual friend Jack, here, got me away from the bad guys. You, uh…probably don't want to hear the details. Wasn't strictly legal. Jack, she doesn't want to hear the details, does she?"

"No," I said.

Janet looked from Julie to me. Her expression tried for trusting and came off wary. "Jack…you don't…you don't work for my *father*, do you?"

"Yes," I said.

The wary expression turned withering, and her nostrils flared, and her teeth were bared when she said, "Let me out," and tried to rise and push by me.

But she was sitting on the inside of the booth and I wouldn't let her, gripping her wrist, making her eyes meet mine.

"Hear me out," I said.

"Why *should* I?"

"So you'll know what's going on, and can make an informed decision."

Her upper lip curled back. "Don't patronize me!"

Across the way Julie was chewing ice from her drink, faintly disgusted. "Oh, brother, Sis...."

"Hear me out," I said, "and I'll let you out."

Still half up, Janet drew in a deep breath, exhaled melodramatically, and settled back in the booth, getting as far away from me as she could, short of knocking a hole through the wall.

Janet folded her arms and looked straight ahead. "My father is a monster. Anybody who does his bidding—"

Julie laughed and said, "Does his *bidding*! Jesus, library lady, cut the guy a break."

The older sister—without looking at me—said, "All right. I'll give you one minute, Jack, and then you either let me out of this booth or I start screaming."

Julie craned her neck out of the booth. "Can I get another Scotch rocks, please? *Thank* you...."

I said to Janet, "Your father hired me to keep an eye on you."

She couldn't help herself; she had to look at me. "Why, in heaven's name?"

"He didn't say."

"Is that why...you...with *Rick*...?"

I was halfway turned in the booth, to face her, and I did my best to keep my words simple, my tone earnest. "I was just supposed to keep track of you. But when that asshole got physical, I—"

"Blew your cover?" she asked bitterly.

"Or," Julie said with a nasty little smile, "maybe climbed under yours, huh, Sis?"

"You be quiet," Janet said.

"You asked about the gun," I said. "This is why."

She was shaking her head, grappling with all this. "You're a, a what…bodyguard? Why would he do that? Why would *my* father hire someone to protect *me*? He doesn't care enough about me to—"

"I've come to that same opinion," I said. "Which is why I think you may be at risk."

Janet didn't seem to hear my last statement, asking, "What…what kind of work do you generally *do* for my father?"

I shrugged. "Troubleshooter."

"Well…that's certainly vague."

"Right."

"I…I really should hate you."

"Probably."

Her chin started quivering and her eyes were getting moist. "You…*goddamn* you. Goddamn *me*—*I* let you into my life."

I nodded. "I know the feeling—I let you into mine."

We looked at each other…

…and suddenly it was fine between us.

Or I was pretty sure it was, and held my hand out.

She gave me her hand and I squeezed it, and Julie, said, "I'm gonna need *way* more Scotch.…"

Our food came soon, and neither Janet nor I did much more than nibble at it. Julie ate about half of hers, but was downing the booze like a pro.

"What did you mean," Janet said, pushing her plate away, "I'm at…risk?"

I pushed my plate away, too. "You're coming into a lot of money, soon, aren't you?"

"Yes.…"

Julie, chewing cheeseburger, said, "And if you flatline, sister dear, guess who gets the gold?"

Janet frowned and then it turned into a smile of disbelief. "Oh, come on…you can't think…our own *father*? Even he wouldn't…*would* he?"

"He would," I said. "It's…a problem."

Janet's eyebrows went up. "A problem?"

"And I know just what to do about it," Julie said. She grabbed the passing waitress and said, "Scotch rocks, double—my sissy sis'll no doubt want a margarita…and how about you, big boy?"

"Coke," I said.

"Give him a twist of line," Julie said, "and let him live dangerously…and keep 'em comin'."

When the waitress had departed, Janet leaned across the booth and took some of the stress out on her sister, saying bitchily, "That's *always* your solution, isn't it? Getting drunk!"

"Or stoned," Julie said, "or laid. But this? This I think calls for drunk."

That was when I noticed someone at the bar, his back to us, as he watched us in the mirror—a brawny big-shouldered guy in gray sweats in his twenties with a close-cropped blonde haircut.

"Excuse me, ladies," I said, and slipped out of the booth.

I sat on the stool next to the guy.

"Hello, DeWayne," I said.

Jonah Green's flunky, his sweatshirt labeled USMC, sipped his beer and said, "Don't talk to me. Are you crazy?"

"That's a matter of opinion. Why are you here, DeWayne? What are you up to?"

DeWayne didn't look at me. He whispered: "Mr. Green has me following that crazy cunt."

"Julie?"

He forgot to whisper this time, saying, "You see any other crazy cunt around here? Mr. Green was afraid she'd screw things up. With the…you know, job."

"*My* job, you mean," I said.

Now he looked at me.

The close-set sky-blue eyes in the oval Clutch Cargo-ish face stared at me unblinkingly; his upper lip approximated a sneer. This was apparently his menacing expression.

"Your *job*," he said nastily, "which apparently includes hangin' out in public with the intended? What are you doin', making contact with—"

I put my hand on his sleeve, and smiled pleasantly. "Leave, DeWayne. Go home. Right now."

"You can't—"

"Do you want to die, DeWayne?"

That stopped him. But then he managed, "You don't—"

"Leave, DeWayne. Or die. Those are the options. Choose."

DeWayne turned away and looked at himself in the mirror. He was bigger than me and younger and he didn't like taking this from a geezer like me—he was trembling, whether with rage or fear or some combo, I couldn't say.

But take it from me he did. He finished the beer, threw a crumpled five-spot on the bar, and headed out the door almost at a trot.

I joined the sisters at the booth.

"Who was that?" Janet asked.

I looked sharply at Julie and shook my head; she, of course, knew who DeWayne was, but she nodded back, almost imperceptibly, and I told her sister, "Nobody, really. Just somebody I thought I knew, but didn't."

"Well, that's funny…" Janet's eyes narrowed, watching where DeWayne had gone. "…I'm pretty sure he was at the library today, just hanging around."

I said nothing.

We spent several hours in the bar, and I asked Janet and Julie lots of questions about their father, about his business, his private and public life. I was fairly subtle about it, and both young women were drinking enough to make my information-gathering relatively inconspicuous. By the time the evening was over, I had plenty of information on Jonah Green and his whereabouts and his patterns.

When it was time to go, I drove Janet home in my rental Ford—she'd had way too many margaritas—while Julie drove her sister's Geo. Julie was pretty drunk, too, but she was used to it, and could navigate well enough. Still, I followed her, to make sure she stayed on the road.

No one tailed us, by the way—just as there'd been no sign of DeWayne in Sneaky Pete's parking lot. Maybe he'd had the sense to follow my advice and survive.

Julie parked the Geo in the lot behind the building and entered through the kitchen to meet us at the apartment's front door. I carried the plastered Janet in my arms like a bride over the threshold into the apartment. Julie, with a display of intense concentration, worked at getting the door night-latched, and made her way to the couch—this time I didn't have to throw her over there.

I carried Janet into the bedroom, left the lights off,

and settled her on top of the covers, taking off her shoes but otherwise letting her sleep there, fully clothed. Already she was snoring gently.

Then I returned to the living room and checked the door, finding it locked and successfully night-latched. I turned off the lights and only a little neon from the street pulsed in—I glanced at the double windows past Janet's comfy chair and footrest; across the way, the windows of my surveillance post were dark and anonymous.

Janet's sister was curled up on the couch, in a fetal position. The heat was on but cool air leeched in those double windows, so I went off and found a blanket and came back and covered Julie with it.

She stirred a little and looked up at me, blinking. "You...you really do love her, don't you, you big jerk?"

I said nothing.

"I thought so," she said, and smiled a little, and then it faded dramatically and she said, "Daddy... Daddy's got something bad planned for Jan, doesn't he?"

"You're on a roll," I said.

I sat on the edge of the couch. I felt fond of this kid, suddenly, and I didn't even want to fuck her. I was getting so goddamn soft.

"Were *you* supposed to do it?" she asked.

"Do what?"

"The bad thing to Janet for Daddy."

I nodded.

"And now…instead…you're going to stop it?"

I touched her lips with a finger. "Get some sleep. You know where the bathroom is? 'Cause you're gonna have to piss like a racehorse."

"I know where the bathroom is.…Some night?"

I frowned at her. "What about 'some night?' "

She got herself more comfortable. "Some night, when you're sittin' all bored and shit…with only my mousy little sis to keep you company…?"

"Yeah?"

"Maybe it'll occur to you."

"What will?"

"That you wound up with the wrong sister."

I stared at her. She did her drunken best to stare back.

"Well," I said, "you are more like what I deserve."

In a goofily good-natured way, she said, "Fuck you," stuck her tongue out and smiled and I tucked her in some more and she was asleep.

My nine millimeter and I went out and prowled the back alley, including checking the parked cars in the lot beyond, where the Geo was. Then I came back in and locked up and returned to the bedroom.

Janet was still on top of the covers, fully dressed,

really sawing logs now, looking not at all glamorous, and incredibly beautiful.

I placed my nine millimeter on the bedstand beside me and stretched out next to the slumbering woman, and lay there in the dark, elbows winged, staring at the ceiling.

Fourteen

The explosion jolted me from deep asleep to fully awake—or the sound of it did, anyway, coming from outside the apartment, to the rear.

Still fully dressed from the night before, I sat up straight, as if from a nightmare; but I was waking *to* a nightmare, and knew it, as I noted the absence of Janet on the rumpled bed next to me.

I grabbed the nine millimeter off the nightstand and bolted toward the noise, which had shifted from full-scale world-rattling boom to lion's roar of fire punctuated by snapping of flames.

The kitchen opened onto a small unenclosed porch and a half-flight of stairs down to the alley, across which lay half a block of metered parking lot, from which the smoke and flames curled a question mark into an overcast morning sky.

Something had exploded in that lot, and it didn't have to be Janet's car, could have been someone else's or something else entirely, gas main maybe, only I knew in my tightened gut that it *did* have to be Janet's car....

I took the steps three at a time and sprinted across to where I could see the Geo, transformed into a twisted mass of steel abstraction decorated with lashing tongues of flame and billowing smoky hands that turned to black fists opening to gray fingers.

Gun ready but with nothing and no one to shoot at, I dropped to my knees as if to pray. But I was not in a prayerful mood—my eyes were ignoring the smoke and taking in various sad, sick sights, from burnt-edged scraps of Janet's brown suede coat to jagged sections of smoldering human flesh.

Not far from where I knelt, half a female arm lay, fingers twitching, just a little, not burnt at all, not even the stump, as if cut off rudely at the elbow and discarded, flung to the asphalt, which was dotted with the red rain of blood. A little ways away, a shoe-less foot had landed on its sole, like the person it belonged to had stepped away, leaving it behind.

Mostly, however, the lot was littered with charred chunks of meat, as if the explosion had been in a butcher's shop, not rigged here in this lot to blow sky-high when the key of the little Geo had been turned.

A sane man might have gone mad.

I went coldly sane, getting to my feet, ignoring the civilians starting to approach the fiery scene, a chorus of *Oh my Gods* and *Oh my Lords* making a frantic premature funeral out of the ungainly pyre. But I was in no mood for ceremony and just turned away and headed for my rental Ford, which wasn't in the lot, parked instead over on the next side street.

In a weird way, the carnage of it made it easier for me to snap into the necessary gear—this was no clean kill, out of my more recent life, but a flashback to Vietnam, where I'd seen any number of friends blown to kibble thanks to land mines and mortar shells. Where you learned to react by retreating inside yourself, but not inviting the emotions in.

So I was in combat mode when I went looking for him.

Homewood had only seven motels, three of them major chains (Holiday Inn, Comfort Inn, Econo Lodge) which was where normally I would have started; but I had a hunch he would be staying close to my digs, since he was obviously keeping an eye on me.

That's why I began where I was staying, at the Homewood Motor Court. I even parked in my own space by my own door, and on foot prowled the line of cabins, looking over the parked vehicles, studying license plates, peering in windows to take in anything showing in front and back seats.

Not many cars were in the spaces, as the motel catered to salesman and other mid-range business people, who were off with their cars pursuing their livelihoods. And when I made his ride, I was relieved to see it parked in the last space belonging to the last cabin at the far end, with no vehicles parked in the nearest four spaces.

That was good.

And the car hadn't been hard to make—on the passenger seat of a Jeep rental were fanned-out magazines, *Soldier of Fortune*, *Black Belt* and several body building rags.

Seeing those had made me smile. Not much of a smile I grant you, a bitter little slash; but a smile. The magazines not only said who this car belonged to, it indicated a guy reading on the job, bored by surveillance work. Usually reading indicates intelligence.

Not this time.

Through the crack of the window, between the wood frame and the drawn blinds, I could see him, hurriedly packing his duffel bag, which was emblazoned with a Marine Corps insignia. The sweats had been replaced by a short-sleeved pale yellow shirt and dark brown slacks and shades-of-brown running shoes. He might have been the president of the Young Republicans on a campus somewhere.

When I went to his door, the nine millimeter was in my left hand, in front of me, so that anyone passing by wouldn't see it.

Not that anyone was passing by. The Homewood Motor Court on this Monday morning was deader than the driver of the Geo. I knew housekeeping didn't come on for another hour. Plenty of time.

The day, I noticed, was crisp and almost cold, the threat of rain making the sky dark. Days like this were surprisingly common in Vietnam, even if muggy hot ones were the norm, in the jungle.

I knocked with my free hand.

The door opened, allowing the room's inhabitant a suspicious look over the night latch, and I was tempted to replay what I'd done to Louis, just shoot the prick in the eye and be done with it...

...but instead I shouldered through, popping the night latch, shoving the door shut behind me with my right hand, and pointing the nine at him with the other.

DeWayne, stunned by the intrusion, belatedly raised the glock he'd had sense enough to take with him answering the door, and with my free hand, I batted it out of his grasp, like a mean sibling slapping a rattle out of a baby's pink fingers.

The gun landed on the nearby bed and bounced off onto the carpeted floor with a clunk, out of view, and reach.

DeWayne's room was larger than mine, a businessman's mini-suite with a meeting area. The framed paintings were abstractions, as if gore had been spattered around in here already.

My reluctant host—a little taller than me, and about as heavy, but overly muscular in a steroid-ish way—just stood there agape, his stubbly blond gyrene haircut seeming to stand on end. His light blue eyes—disturbingly long-lashed pretty eyes, really, feminine in the midst of all that otherwise rugged-jaw masculinity—had the same startled expression they'd worn when I slipped in beside DeWayne in his car outside the Log Cabin, a few months ago.

Right before he thanked me for not killing him and I locked him in his trunk—remember?

I shoved my nine millimeter in my waistband. But that didn't seem to make DeWayne feel any better—in fact, he seemed unnerved, perhaps because I appeared so calm.

And I was in fact calm, entirely matter-of-fact and unemotional. Which he should have been thankful for. If I hadn't slipped into my battle zone, he'd have been dead now.

I asked, in a purely conversational tone, "What the fuck was that about back there, DeWayne?"

DeWayne blinked.

I raised my eyebrows. "The *car*, DeWayne? The one you rigged that blew up this morning? Oh, but maybe you didn't hang around to watch."

His mouth twitched, like it couldn't decide whether to smile or frown or scream.

"In which case," I continued affably, "you'll be pleased to know it did go off and blow Janet Wright's car to hell and gone—driver and all."

His expression tightened into defensiveness.

"Well, *somebody* had to do it! After you've been *farting* around for *days!*"

"...How long have you been watching me, DeWayne?"

He shook his head. "I told you—I followed Mr. Green's slutty little princess here. She wasn't supposed to be part of the mix, you know."

My hands were on my hips. "But, then, neither were you, DeWayne. Was *that* the plan? Let me do the job, then get rid of the loose end?"

"No! Hell, no! I told you—"

My eyes slitted. "I told *you*, last night. This is *my* job."

DeWayne risked getting in my face, just a little: "Which included *fucking* her, I suppose? Where is that in your job description, old man? You ain't exactly a stealth missile."

I drew in a breath, let it out. "Car bomb," I said.

"Huh?"

"Car bomb. Yeah. *That'll* play as an accident."

My remark took the boldness out of him, replacing it with chagrin. "Yeah, well...things were...out of control. I made a...a *pre-emptive* strike. But you don't need to worry."

My eyebrows went up again. "I don't?"

He smirked humorlessly. "No—you'll get your money."

"...Well, isn't that thoughtful. And then there's all the credit—I'll get that, too." Finally I frowned at him. "Jesus, DeWayne—I've been seen all over town with that woman!"

Now his eyebrows went up. "Is that *my* fault?"

"No," I admitted. "That's my fault. Blowing her up in her car, that would be yours."

He backed away, hands half-up, saying, "Listen, I'm sorry I stepped on your fuckin' toes...but I had orders to follow...and now I got a plane to catch."

Cautiously DeWayne returned to the duffel bag he was packing; his gun was over there on the floor, somewhere. Part of me wished he would go for it, please go for it, right now, *go for it....*

"I need to finish packing," he said, doing his best to sound casual, gesturing to the bag. "You got a problem with that?"

I shook my head. "Not at all—but why don't you pack after your shower?"

"My what?"

"When's your plane, DeWayne?"

Various vague gestures accompanied his reply: "Two hours from now, but I got to drive over to—"

"You got plenty of time for a quick shower."

He stared at me like I was a raving madman, even though I was not raving. "What the *fuck*...?"

Slowly but steadily, I removed the nine from my

waistband and pointed it at him. "Take your clothes off, DeWayne."

His eyes and nostrils flared, the short blond hair damn near bristling. "The *hell!*"

I gestured a little with the gun, not vaguely. "Go on and strip....I'm locking you in the bathroom so you don't follow me."

He shook his head, wild-eyed, blurting, "I'm not gonna fucking *follow* your ass!"

"That's right," I said. "Because I'm locking *your* ass in the can, and taking your clothes. That'll give me the lead I need, to get out of this podunk."

DeWayne sighed. Shook his head. Opened his palms placatingly. "*Please*, buddy. Come on, will ya? What the hell'd I ever do to—"

"Skivvies and all, DeWayne. All the way."

"...Christ." His eyes popped with alarm. "Oh, Christ, you *fell* for her!"

"*Now*, DeWayne...."

Frantic, pawing the air, he said, "Look, you can't blame me for this. It was Mr. *Green*. Once a guy like Mr. Green decides you're dead, you're fucking dead! *You* know that! She was a dead man walkin'—I was just the means to an end, and if it wasn't me, it coulda been any—"

"Spare me the horseshit, DeWayne, and strip the fuck down."

DeWayne slumped in defeat.

Moving in slow motion, he began unbuttoning the pale yellow shirt, then—and this was admirable, he didn't telegraph it all—swept a curving martial-arts kick around that popped the nine millimeter right out of my grasp.

The gun slid across the carpet and hid under a chest of drawers, as if wanting nothing to do with any of what was about to come.

Shaking my head and smiling, I said, "This isn't really necessary, DeWayne."

He went into a karate-school stance that I wish I could say looked hokey, but it didn't—he was a muscular young ex-Marine who clearly knew his shit, and it hadn't all come out of *Black Belt* magazine, either.

"That's *my* call, Pops!"

It was my turn to sigh.

"Go ahead, kid. Take your best shot."

And he did, kicking high and out, aiming at my head. If it had connected, I'd likely have been dead, my neck broken.

So I ducked it.

DeWayne reared back, confusion coloring his face, and paused for a moment.

"Couldn't we just skip this, son?"

Teeth bared, he tried again, rushing me with a flurry of blows, bladed hands here, fists there, and I ducked and slipped and dodged.

He followed me as I circled away, and when he high-kicked, I got out of the way, and his running-shod foot broke a mirror over the dresser, shards raining noisily. I circled back and he charged me and I stepped aside and he busted off the top half of a chair, making a stool out of it.

Finally he began to lose his cool, which isn't a part of any martial arts program I know of; but you couldn't blame the poor bastard—I was frustrating the hell out of him, avoiding his every blow, never raising my hands. I didn't even bother taunting him, ignoring anything he said to me ("Stand still, gramps!") and, with the mini-suite half demolished, he went for broke with a flying kick that I stepped aside for, and he crashed to the floor with a whump.

I just stood there, arms folded causually, not having broken a sweat, while he got to his feet, then bent over, exhausted, panting, pausing with his hands on his thighs.

"*Je*-sus," he said, trying hard to catch his breath, still hunkered over, "*Je*-sus…why don't you…you… *fuckin'*…fuckin' *do* something?"

I slammed a fist into the side of his head, connecting with his ear and temple, and the big guy went down, in a pile.

He wasn't out, but he was out of it, and when he finally looked back up at me, pitifully—his face red and fully sweat-beaded, his ear bleeding from the side of his head where I'd hit him—the nine millimeter was back in my hand, its dark eye staring him down.

"See, DeWayne? You do need a shower."

That made him slump some more, as if all the remaining energy just drained out of him, but he was still breathing hard. He sat there, kind of sideways, his legs sprawled, like a cripple whose faith-healing hadn't taken.

"Just," he said, and heaved a couple breaths, and then tried again: "Just *do* it. Awright? Just...fucking... *kill* me."

I shook my head and my expression was fairly pleasant. "I'm not gonna kill you, kid. Strip."

Allowing himself the luxury of being reassured, DeWayne somehow got to his feet—it was kind of like watching one of those demolition-of-a-building film clips played backward, a structure reassembling itself—and once again, back to slow motion, he began to unbutton his shirt.

No tricks.

No attacks.

No surprises.

All he did was perform the least interesting striptease I have ever witnessed, discreetly turning his back to me at the finish, his arms—muscular, decorated with various USMC tattoos—hanging as slack as his muscular buttocks were taut.

He glanced back at me for his orders.

"The shitter," I told him.

And I marched the dejected DeWayne into the bathroom. The young soldier wasn't looking for an escape route, or at least I didn't think he was. He seemed relatively unafraid, probably figuring I'd have killed him by now, if that was the point.

Just inside the cramped bathroom, he again looked over his shoulder and said, "You mind a little friendly advice? Don't tangle asses with Mr. Green. I know you're not happy about how this went down. But just…go your own way."

"Semper fi, Mac," I said.

There was no tub, just a shower stall with the familiar pebbled glass.

He swallowed. "Now what?"

"Get in."

This seemed to alarm him, and his head swivelled on the muscular neck. "What the fuck for?"

Keeping it low-key, sticking the nine back in my waistband, I said, "I'm going to wedge something against the door, and lock you in. Buy me some time."

"I told you I wouldn't—"

"Right. Get in."

Compliantly, DeWayne opened the door and stepped in the stall, and stood there with a good-size dick hanging and an expression that was neither moronic nor intelligent—perfect makings for a Marine.

"And?" he asked.

"And," I said, "be careful, DeWayne. You'd be surprised how many accidents happen in the bathroom."

He squinted at me, not getting that, and I used both hands to slam his head into the shower stall wall, with all the force I could muster.

The sound of his skull cracking wasn't loud but it was distinct, and perhaps DeWayne even had time to hear it; either way, he was already dead, wide-eyed and frozen in time, as he slid slowly down the wall, leaving a bloody snail-smear behind him.

He sat there quietly, pretty blue eyes staring into eternity, his limbs like kindling, as I unwrapped a motel bar of soap and then flipped the thing to land near DeWayne's big dead feet. I'd been careful to bash his head into the wall on the side where my fist had hit him earlier, the only blow I'd delivered in our hand-to-hand exercise.

Then I turned on the shower, nice and hot (to make time of death a mystery), and let the steamy spray do its tapdance on the corpse.

I hadn't touched much in the room—the soap would be worn down by the needles of water—so I didn't have much cleaning up to do.

Not in Homewood I didn't.

Fifteen

The massive ornate granite gravestone was a family affair, reading on top:

MARY ANN GREEN	*JONAH ALLEN GREEN*
(1940–1985)	*(1938–)*
Beloved Wife and Mother	

and below:

JANET ANN GREEN	*JULIA SUSAN GREEN*
(1975–2005)	*(1985–)*
Cherished Daughter	

From my post behind some rich man's mausoleum, I couldn't see that lettering; but I'd been at the cemetery since last night, and had taken in the inscription by moonlight. I'd been by far the first to get here for Janet Green's farewell appearance.

Her casket, on the other hand, I could easily see from here, my position elevated enough to view the copper capsule, which had already been deposited in the ground, the metallic tubes of the lowering device still in place. I'd skipped the funeral, not really feeling wanted, and the graveside ceremony was long since over.

The morning was crisp and cold with moving clouds that sent phantom-like shadows gliding across the snow-brushed grounds of Oak Brook Memorial Cemetery. The mourners had drifted away, though a few lingered to pay their respects to the grieving father—Jonah Green, in his dark gray Saville Row topcoat, saying nothing, just nodding severe thanks with that square head with its square jaw, the short-cut bristly haircut giving him a vaguely military cast.

And now Green was a solitary figure at his daughter's graveside, standing with hands figleafed before him, head lowered, making a mournful picture that maybe, maybe not, had some real feeling in it.

Who knows—could be there was some humanity left in this son of a bitch. Could be he felt a pang about killing his oldest daughter to gain more of his late wife's money. He certainly seemed truly mournful as he bent to collect a handful of piled graveside dirt, then standing and tossing it in. Even from where I was tucked back watching, I could hear the soil shower the casket like hard, brief rain.

The final cars drew away, leaving only the Cadillac hearse and a second vehicle, a BMW. The mourners, other than Green himself, were gone. The only company remaining was keeping a respectful distance, but staying alert: half a dozen scattered security men in dark raincoats and sunglasses, peppered here and there on the periphery, keeping in touch via headsets.

Not that I'd give them high marks, since I'd easily kept out of their sight when they did their advance sweep of the cemetery, early this morning. Nor were they aware that the uniformed chauffeur assigned to drive the hearse was currently tossed in the back of the vehicle wrapped in more duct tape than a leaky drainpipe.

Which was why—when the liveried "chauffeur" in cap and sunglasses approached Jonah Green at the graveside—neither the millionaire nor any of his six security boys thought anything of it.

I stepped to Green's side and, head still lowered, he said, "Just a few more minutes, Roger—I'm...I'm not ready just yet."

"My final payment hasn't reached my off-shore account," I said, removing the sunglasses and tucking them in a breast pocket. "Why the delay?"

Green looked at me sharply with those money-color eyes, but he'd been to the rodeo a few times himself, so his surprise and alarm quickly faded to a weary bitter smile.

"Quarry. Nice of you to come."

My cap was in hand now, respectfully. "Wouldn't miss it."

He turned back to the grave, looked down into it.

"As for your payment, well…you didn't do the work, did you?"

"You interfered with the job. Or, anyway, that dope of yours did."

The square head swung toward me again, his forehead creased with a frown but his mouth a straight line. "Was that really necessary? What you did to DeWayne?"

"Not as necessary as you killing your daughter…. Nice turnout today."

He stared down into the grave again. "Not many of them knew Janet—they were kind to pay their respects."

"Where was her sister? Was Julie at the funeral? Didn't spot her at the graveside service."

He was maintaining an admirable cool; on the other hand, he knew we had that security crew of his, all around us. Still, he was well aware what I was capable of, and a certain tension, even nervousness, flicked in and around his eyes.

"I thought maybe *you* knew where Julie was," he said. His tone was surface cordial, underlying contemptuous. "Hell, I thought I might get another phone call from you, wanting more unmarked money."

"That hurts."

He lifted his shoulders and set them down again. "All I know is, Julie's dropped out of sight."

"Well, maybe she's afraid Daddy might be thinking of doubling up on the trust fund action."

Green glared at me. "I would *never* harm that girl."

"Sorry. How could I ever think such a thing?"

"I adore that child!"

"I was just thinking maybe it was a set-up all along—that maybe you engineered that snatch.... After all, you said yourself you had certain business connections, in those circles."

He sneered. "Don't be an ass."

"Makes sense—the wild child dies, Daddy inherits. But I came along and screwed it up for you. So Plan B was daughter number one."

He was shaking his head, looking out past the gravestone, at the world beyond; mostly all you could see of that world was more gravestones, some trees, and the gray tombstones of suburban Oak Brook's business buildings.

"You're wrong, Quarry—though why I should care what a creature like you thinks is beyond me."

"There I agree with you."

He swung toward me with his eyes slits, his face grooved grimly. "I was not responsible for that kidnapping—no. Julie has potential. She has fire. Spirit. She's just…going through a phase."

I nodded toward the hole in the ground. "So is your other daughter—it's called decomposition."

He leaned toward me, eyes furious, face otherwise blank; he'd been keeping his voice down, and his movements small, obviously not anxious to start a fracas between his boys and me, out here in front of God and everybody, with himself in the middle.

"What the hell do you want, Quarry? The rest of your money?"

"That would be a start."

He shook his head, quietly disgusted. "Well, I don't want a scene, here. Can you understand that? Can you have a little respect for the dead?"

"Did you really say that, or am I hallucinating?"

"Fuck you. Just go. Go, and I'll make your god-damn money happen."

I said nothing. Now I was the one looking down into that hole in the ground. "...You warned me that she didn't deserve it."

He winced. "What—Janet?...No, she was a nice enough young woman. Harmless. Silly, naive, in how she viewed the world, but...anyway. She was lost to me. Lost to me long ago."

"Oh?"

He had a distant expression now. For the first time I detected a genuine sense of loss in him, if edged with a bitter anger. "To her...to her I represented everything bad about this country."

I shrugged. "Kids."

He glared at me again. "She had a nothing life, Quarry—a librarian."

He said "librarian" the way another disappointed father might have said "shoplifter" or "prostitute."

He was saying, "I have a small empire to maintain—thousands of employees, with families, depending on me for their paychecks."

"Hey," I said. "You sacrificed a child. Worked for God."

He winced again. Sighed grandly. Said, "Go—just fucking go. Do that, cause no more trouble, and there'll be a nice bonus for you—not that you deserve shit."

"Oh," I said, "I deserve shit…but your daughter didn't. Mr. Green…Jonah? Okay I call you 'Jonah'? I feel a certain closeness to you."

"Are you insane?"

"Is that a rhetorical question? See, I always assumed the people I killed were marked for death, anyway, and I was a means to a predetermined end."

Green—studying me now, clearly wondering where this was going—said, "I gathered as much."

"People I put down probably did deserve it…or anyway put themselves in the gunsights, one way or another. By something they'd done."

"Of course."

"But Janet…" I smiled at him, only it didn't really

have much to do with smiling. "...she was a good person. A decent person. She didn't deserve to die."

He bit the words off acidly: "I *told* you that going *in*."

"Yeah. My bad." I shook my head, laughed a little. "You know, Mr. Green, in a long and varied career in the killing business, I've never encountered anyone quite like you—ready to kill your own daughter for another chunk of the family fortune."

The security guys had started getting suspicious, taking notice of this unlikely long conversation between chauffeur and boss. From the corners of my eyes, I saw them talking into their headsets; it was like being stalked by air traffic controllers.

"Walk away," Green said softly. "Your money will be doubled, and—since we've come to find each other so distasteful—we don't ever have to have contact again."

I raised a forefinger, gently, and nodded toward the names carved in granite. "One little thing—you're going to need to revise that headstone."

"Really?"

"That wasn't Janet in that car."

He took it like a slap. Time stuttered, and his mouth dropped open, his eyes flaring; but despite this obvious alarm, the millionaire went into immediate denial, saying, "Well, certainly it was Janet."

"No. She's alive and well and somewhere you can't find her."

"You *are* insane...."

"See, Jonah, your girls got a little tipsy, the night before," I said, "and next morning Julie put on one of her sister's coats...it was chilly...and went out to get the car, to bring it around to give her hungover sister a ride to work."

His face turned white, like the dead skin a blister leaves.

I went on: "I liked Julie. You're right—she did have fire. Particularly at the end, there."

"No," Green said, and he tried to smile, tried to shrug it off. "No, I don't believe you....This is some sick—"

"Hey, what's the difference, Dad? Trust fund money is trust fund money."

That was when he lost it, and rushed me, reaching out with curled fingers to try to strangle me, I guess. And he was a big man, bigger than me, and powerful, despite the years he had on me. I could hear the security guys, not bothering with headsets now, flat-out yelling, on the run.

But then I had Jonah Green locked in an embrace, my arms pinning his, and I was close enough to kiss the bastard.

I grinned into his fucking face and said, "That's not *all* you'll need to revise on that headstone...."

Then I shifted, holding him by one arm, and I let him sense the nose of the nine millimeter in his gut, just so he could know it was coming, and I fired twice. The sounds were muffled by his clothing and his body, and were like coughs, not even loud enough to echo.

Stepping back, releasing him from my embrace, I watched with pleasure as he stumbled back, open-mouthed, awkward and—arms windmilling—tripped over the metal tubing of the lowering device and tumbled backward into his daughter's grave, smacking the metal of the casket, hard.

Now *that* echoed.

The security guys had me surrounded and I wheeled, going from face to face, smiling easily, my gun in hand pointed skyward, my other hand up, too.

"No need, fellas!" I said. "You're off the payroll. Time to hit the unemployment lines...."

They began trading glances, considering my words—after all, they had just seen the prick they worked for gut-shot, twice, and presumably they'd been told I was dangerous, I was in fact why they were fucking here, so I was clearly a guy with a gun who, if confronted, would take some of them down.

But Jonah Green was a tough old bird, and badly wounded though he was, bleeding from the mouth, front of his clothing splotched with blood, he was nonetheless alive, and trying to crawl, claw his way up and out of the ground.

When his head popped up in that grave, his men jumped a little; and maybe I did, too.

"Shoot him!" Green cried, gargling blood a little as he did. He was holding onto a metal tube of the lowering device. "Cut him *down!*"

When the guns started appearing in the hands of the security men, I moved out, ducking back behind the massive Green family gravestone, firing the nine millimeter at the only guy in sunglasses, headset and raincoat on that side of the world.

The guy took it in the head, and fell backward, like a narcoleptic suddenly asleep, but leaving blood mist behind.

With the headstone as cover, I took out the two closest ones, and each did an individualistic death dance, though with much in common—spurting blood, tumbling to the snowy grass—while the surviving trio went scrambling for cover, behind other gravestones.

I used the rest of the clip exchanging gunfire with them, bullets careening and *whing*ing off the granite headstones, carving nicks and holes. But they were spread out just enough to make my task difficult.

Concentrating on one at a time, I took the nearest to me when he slipped his head out to take aim, my shot sending him back, sprawling against another gravestone, staring in surprise with both eyes and the new hole between them.

We all stayed put while shadows chased each other under the cold cloud-shifting sky. Wind riffled branches and stubborn leaves whispered and some of us were breathing hard, but not me. I felt fine, and was thinking what a tempting goal the Caddy hearse on the hillock made.

The keys to it were in my pocket, but the remaining security boys were between me and the vehicle. I needed to get closer.

Plus, I had to get a better angle on the other shooters, so I quickly reloaded and took a chance, breaking cover to sprint for a better position. I heard three shots but none of them came close to catching me, and I flopped behind another headstone, alive and well.

"*Now*," I heard one of them say, and peeked out and saw them both running for new positions, in opposite directions.

I could only choose one. He had almost made it to cover when my shot caught him in the side of the head and he went tumbling on now useless legs.

The other guy had found a new spot, a good one, behind a massive affair with a granite angel perched on top. He and I both had good cover now, and we traded shots and chipped pieces off our respective headstones and didn't get anywhere.

But I could hear him breathing—breathing hard—and, hell, I wasn't even winded. I was older by fifteen years easy, but I was a swimmer, remember; this guy must have been a smoker, and that can kill your ass.

So I had that advantage, if nothing else. Listening carefully, I could hear him doing a speed-reload, and I was grinning as I popped up, blasting away at his headstone, specifically at the decorative angel, emptying the clip.

The cupid-like statue flew apart, into fragments, bursting into the guy's face. He cried out as he reared back, and I took the opportunity to sprint for that hearse, shoving in a fresh clip as I did.

My opponent was too busy blinking away dust and chips, his face flecked with shards of granite, to get a good aim at my fleeing figure.

Still on the run, I took a look back and thought *what the hell* and aimed and fired.

He, too, took a bullet in the head and fell backward, haloed in blood, flung between stones, just as dead as anybody already underground.

I got into the hearse and started it up, then swung around onto the little gravel roadway, where the windshield gave me a view on a tableau that would have been memorable even without the scattered bodies of the security team...

...Jonah Green emerging from his daughter's grave, crawling up over those metal lowering tubes, the front of him shot up, but definitely still alive, and then he was on his feet, albeit weaving like a damn drunk.

He teetered at the edge of the grave, his back to it—unsteady yes, but standing, and the square face set with almost crazed determination.

To do what? I wondered. *Survive? Kill me?*

So I floored the fucking thing, found a lane between gravestones, and went charging across the grass, and he must have heard the engine's roar because he turned toward me, the determination shifting to terror, as the hearse bore down.

I clipped him good as I passed, garnering a truly satisfying crunch, and sent him toppling back into the grave, landing to make another metallic, echoing *thud*.

Slamming on the brakes, I hopped out, nine millimeter in my fist, and ran to the grave, where Green—down in there on top of his daughter's copper coffin, arms in crucifixion position—looked up at me with the money-color eyes wide open and staring.

But he didn't see me. He was very, very dead.

Which was a bit of a disappointment, because I would just as soon have shot him some more.

Time to go.

I was paused just long enough to dump the duct-taped mummy of the real hearse driver, and got back in a vehicle that looked little the worse for wear for having just run a guy down.

This time I didn't floor it, just cruised out of the cemetery in my chauffeur's uniform, my hands on the wheel of the hearse, passing assorted Oak Brook Memorial personnel coming out of hiding, scurrying along the periphery, now that the shooting was over.

Sixteen

Oak Brook Memorial was easing into spring, the snow gone, the grass greening, but this could just as easily have been November as late March. Once again cloud cover threw shadows on the cemetery, but this time they more or less stayed put, just lending a blue-gray cast to the tombstone-studded landscape.

The gravesite still looked fresh, the unusual procedure of the contents of a grave needing to be shifted one to the right making it look like two relatively recent burials had taken place.

A correction had also been made on the massive granite gravestone. Whether this was a fresh slab, or whether tombstone cutters have their own kind of Liquid Paper, I couldn't tell you.

At any rate, it now read:

MARY ANN GREEN	*JONAH ALLEN GREEN*
(1940–1985)	*(1938–2005)*
Beloved Wife and Mother	*Husband and Father*

and below:

JANET ANN GREEN　　JULIA SUSAN GREEN

(1975–)　　　　(1985–2005)

Cherished Daughter

A woman in a black wool coat, black slacks and red sweater knelt to place a floral wreath at one of the graves, taking care to position it just right. She lowered her head and, apparently, began to pray.

I let Janet finish the mumbo jumbo before I wandered down from my surveillance post behind that mausoleum on the hillock, and when she finally stood, I was at her side.

At first, she was startled—couldn't blame her: she hadn't seen me for several months, not since I'd shuffled her out of Homewood and onto a plane. But very soon her expression turned calm, almost serene.

"Your friend Gary," she said, "was very nice."

I nodded. "Florida makes a nice getaway in the winter."

She was looking at me the way a mother checks a kid getting over the measles. "He wouldn't tell me anything about you."

And once again, I was glad I hadn't killed my old Vietnam buddy, after getting drunk and spilling my guts to him, that time. Even a prick like me can use a friend now and again.

"His wife's nice, too," she said conversationally.

"Ruthie. Yeah. A peach."

"She doesn't know *anything* about you."

"Yeah, well, I'm an enigma wrapped up in a riddle."

She almost smiled. "What now?"

My eyes met hers, and it wasn't the easiest thing I ever did. "We can do it two ways. I can tell you everything…or nothing."

She thought about that.

Then Janet said, "If you tell me everything…" She gestured toward the gravestone. "…will I be next?"

"No. But you were supposed to be."

She frowned. "My father…?"

My eyes remained locked with hers. "Can you live with it?"

She sighed; looked away; shivered—it was still cold, after all—and folded her arms to herself, her hands in leather gloves. Her gaze lingered on the gravestone and then slowly shook her head.

"You mean, what Daddy did? Or what you've done?…What you might have done?"

"All that," I said.

Her eyes came to mine again. "Or do you mean… could I live with *you*?"

I said nothing.

Our eyes remained locked.

"Your call," I said, and I walked away, moving across the cloud-shadowed landscape, finding my way between tombstones, heading up that hill.

I could feel her eyes on me, but she did not call out.

So I was back where we began, in my A-frame, still managing Sylvan Lodge for Gary Petersen, and caught up in getting the place ready for the new season. Next week staff would be in, and I'd have to start dealing with being around people again.

Harry and Louis hadn't shown up yet. Perhaps they were tangled in something down at the bottom of the lake, and were doing me the favor of feeding fish and turning to skeletons. I still felt that if their bloated remains did decide to float to the surface, their mob background would keep any heat off an innocent civilian like me.

And it was a big lake. Sylvan Lodge was only one little notch on it.

Of course, staying on at Sylvan at all was itself a risk—Jonah Green had found me here, hadn't he? Come walking right into my world?

But Jonah was dead; he wouldn't be crawling up out of that grave again, not even on Judgement Day. And he had no doubt been discreet in his inquiries about me—he had to be, since he was a selfish sociopath plotting his own daughter's death, which generally calls for discretion.

Thing was, I was just too goddamn old to start over. And I liked it here. I liked the cabin, and Gary, and the (must I use this word?) lifestyle. In the unlikely event that assholes with guns came looking for me, they would find another asshole with a gun who would kill them.

A rationalization, sure; but I could live with it.

You will be relieved, I'm sure, to learn that my problem with insomnia was a thing of the past—I was sleeping long and deep with my only problem that low backache I had on waking, but walking over and swimming and using the Jacuzzi and doing a few stretches got rid of that.

Still, old habits die hard, and three nights before the Sylvan staff was about to arrive, a sound woke me—a clatter out there that was not fucking Santa Claus, and my waking thought was that somebody had broken in.

Funny how I can sleep so deep, but the littlest goddamn noise and I'm suddenly wide awake, alert as a butt-fucked sailor; I sat up in bed, the nine millimeter from the nightstand tight in my hand.

Call it paranoia, if you will. But when you make a career out of killing people, you tend to think the worst.

And something was definitely rattling around out in my kitchen.

I crept through the darkened cabin and saw a little light was on in there. Gun in hand, I slipped in and flipped the overhead light switch.

"Shit!" Janet said, wincing at the flood of illumination.

As usual, she was wearing one of my shirts, legs bare, her long dark blonde hair fetchingly tousled, and she was bending down, looking in the refrigerator. She straightened like an exclamation point. "Are you trying to scare me to death?"

I lowered the gun. "No."

She shut the refrigerator door and turned to me, her expression innocently apologetic now. "Did I wake you?"

I sat at the kitchen table and put the nine millimeter down in front of me, like it was a fork or a spoon. Rubbed my face with two hands.

"I sleep light," I said.

"So I've noticed." She stood next to me and touched my shoulder and smiled in that way that meant she wanted something. "There's not a damn thing in that fridge....Would you do me a favor?"

"Who do you want me to kill?"

She gave me a reproving look. One might say, a wifely look.

Then her expression softened and she asked, "Could you please make a convenience store run?"

I just looked at her. She had no notion of the significance of her request.

Janet gestured around the little kitchen, like a disaster survivor talking to a reporter about the damage. "We have cereal here, but no milk. I can make a little list....Would you mind, terribly? And, uh—this is embarrassing, but..."

And now the poor-pitiful-me look.

"...would you mind picking up some Tampax?"

I let out a long sigh, pushed out the chair, stood, and said, "No problem."

She touched my face and kissed my cheek. "You are *so* sweet...."

Maybe I was.

But I took the nine millimeter with me.

Author's Afterword

This is the sixth novel about the hitman who calls himself Quarry.

The first was mostly written around 1973 at the University of Iowa, where I was studying in the Writers Workshop; it was published by Berkley Books in 1975 as *The Broker*, though my preferred title was *Quarry* (and it's been reprinted as such). Three novels followed in quick succession, at the publisher's request, and that seemed to be it.

In the mid-'80s, the success of my Nathan Heller series inspired a couple of editors at a couple of houses to ask me to revive Quarry and my other early character, the retired thief Nolan. So I did a Quarry novel called *Primary Target* for Louis Wilder at Foul Play Press, and a Nolan called *Spree* for Michael Seidman at TOR. These were not intended as relaunchings of those series, but a revisitation by an author in midstream of the creations that had launched him.

Over the years, Quarry has built a certain cult following (I always caution enthusiastic readers to remember the Donald E. Westlake definition of a "cult" success: "Seven readers short of the author making a living") and, more recently, I've written an occasional short story about him. Not long ago, those stories and *Primary Target* were collected by Five Star as *Quarry's Greatest Hits*.

One of the stories, "A Matter of Principal," has taken on a kind of life of its own. Of any short story of mine, over my thirty-some-year career, it has been reprinted most often, and was even selected by Jeff Deaver as one of the best *noir* short stories of the 20th century. I have no idea why. I wrote it on assignment, one afternoon, with no plot outline— just working from something that had happened the night before when I made a midnight run to a convenience store and saw a burly guy buying tampons.

Perhaps half a dozen years ago, a young filmmaker in California, Jeffrey Goodman, discovered the short story and began getting after me to give him permission to make a film out of it. For a while I kind of shrugged this off, but eventually he wore me down—I liked the short films Jeffrey sent me by way of samples, and I liked his persistence, too.

Coincidentally, I'd begun working as an independent filmmaker myself here in my native Iowa. This I'd done out of frustration about having so many things optioned by Hollywood but seeing nothing made (this was before "Road to Perdition," obviously).

So I finally told Jeffrey "yes," on two conditions.

The first condition was that I would write the screenplay for the short film, which Jeffrey intended to be a showcase piece for the festival circuit. The second was that I would be the executive producer and would have input in post-production (I did not want to be on set, because I knew I would interfere). Jeffrey was as good as his word, and in particular my suggestions on editing the piece had a nice effect on the final cut.

Jeffrey's short film "A Matter of Principal" became quite successful in the festival world, winning several and an official selection of several others. A year later, I combined Jeffrey's film into an anthology of short films written (and otherwise directed) by me, entitled "Shades of Noir," and that did well in several festivals, also. That anthology film eventually expanded to include my documentary "Mike Hammer's Mickey Spillane," and this novel is officially a tie-in to the Neo-Noir DVD release of the feature-length version of "Shades of Noir."

But this book would not exist if Hard Case Crime

editor Charles Ardai hadn't been kind enough to contact me about contributing to his first slate of books—he specifically wanted to reprint my Nolan novel *Blood Money*, which was the direct sequel to another of my Iowa City college-era books, *Bait Money* (both were published in 1973 by the now long-defunct Curtis Books). I suggested the two novels be published as one longer book, *Two for the Money*, and Charles generously agreed to put it out in that form.

Then Charles asked me to do an original novel for Hard Case—specifically, a Quarry. My previous commitments made that tough, but—knowing that Charles had lured the master of paperback painters, Robert McGinnis, into doing a cover or two for Hard Case—I said, "Sure, I'll do an original book, Charles... *if* you get me McGinnis for the cover."

It was a typical flip, kidding-on-the-square remark of mine—after all, McGinnis is the artist behind the classic Sean Connery "James Bond" movie posters!—but I'll be damned if Charles didn't call me up and say, yes, he had lined "Bob McGinnis" up for the cover of the new Quarry.

Having Mr. McGinnis's brilliant work adorning a book of mine is one of the happiest events of my career—the Mickey Spillane/Gold Medal Books era during which Robert McGinnis first flourished had everything to do with the perditious road I chose to spend my life going down. I thank Charles, and Bob, for their kindness and generosity.

The book itself is an expansion of that much-anthologized short story, "A Matter of Principal," with a dab from another Quarry tale, "Guest Services." The reason behind this approach is two-fold. For various personal agendas, both Charles and I wanted to make this book a tie-in to the release of "Shades of Noir" on DVD. But, also, filmmaker Jeffrey Goodman had decided he wanted to make a feature-length film version of "A Matter of Principal."

So the combined result of Charles's request for a new Quarry novel, and Jeffrey's request for an expanded version of "A Matter of Principal," was this novel (and a screenplay version). Whether Jeffrey and I are fortunate enough to see this story brought in its entirety to the screen remains to be seen—well, I hope it will be seen; in any case, I feel fortunate that Jeffrey created a wonderful short film that led to this one last Quarry adventure.

Editor Ardai, by the way, is responsible for the title, *The Last Quarry*. (The title of the short story was just a silly pun on "principle," and has confused readers, editors and viewers of the short film ever since. Not every writer can lay claim to causing so much confusion with so casual a stroke of the word processor.) Thanks for that, too, Charles.

Is this the last Quarry?

Well, Quarry and I are whores at heart, so anything is possible. But should I ever write any more stories about this man—who ties with Nate Heller as my favorite among my characters—the action will in all likelihood pre-date this novel. This, in my mind, is indeed the last story about him. He is, after all, retired and in the care of a good woman.

The most perverse conclusion I can envision for Quarry, you see, is a happy ending.

Max Allan Collins
Muscatine, Iowa
September 2005